Timeless Heart Reunion

Timeless Heart Reunion

DeLora Conley-Walls

THREE SKILLET

TIMELESS HEART REUNION, Conley-Walls, DeLora

First Edition

The Reunion Series, Book 2

 THREE SKILLET

www.ThreeSkilletPublishing.com

Cover by Farley L Dunn

ISBN: 978-1-943189-62-5

— 1 —

"WELCOME TO SHADETREE Assisted Living Center."

Beth Taylor covered the phone receiver and called out the words brightly. She was finishing a call, and she sat behind her broad, mahogany Chippendale desk. Her nails were freshly done in glossy gumball pink, and her blonde bob just hit her shoulders. She'd completed high school forty years earlier, but except for a light web of lines around her eyes and lips, she'd been told she was as attractive as the day she'd received her diploma.

As she spoke into the phone, Beth opened her devotional for the day, *Following in the Footprints of Jesus,* and glanced at the morning's words from 1 John 1:9. The book helped her keep her sense of balance when she faced difficult situations, and she made a point to read in it every day. "If we confess our sins, he is faithful and just to forgive us our sins, and to cleanse us from all unrighteousness."

Beth breathed a little easier. *Forgive us our sins.* That was something she could use daily. She'd barely finished her greeting and disconnected when she looked up and caught sight of the well-dressed man coming through the door.

Her heart plummeted.

Beth rubbed her hands together to find her palms were suddenly moist, and her stomach felt like a hundred butterflies had just been released. This was a man she'd never intended to face again, and now he walked her direction. Her high school fortieth reunion was planned in a little over a week, so she should have anticipated him, but he'd never attended a single reunion in the past 39 years, so why should she have expected him now? She had conveniently blocked him out of her mind, like one does old numbers on a cell phone. If blocked long enough, the number seems forgotten. Now, here he was, as tall as she remembered, although the gray at his temples was new. He was still lean, though that lanky, high school trimness was gone. Rugged, with long legs and wide shoulders, he carried the look of a man who knew what he wanted in life, not just a teenager curious about everything. His jeans were pressed and covered the tops of polished alligator boots. A brown leather blazer was open at the waist, revealing a wide turquoise buckle.

She felt her breath quicken as she stood and held out her hand. Her motion was automatic and professional, despite the jelly in her knees. She wouldn't let him see how she felt. She couldn't. She would be poised and efficient, a professional woman in a professional environment.

She took a deep breath as he drew closer. She steeled herself, reminding herself she was more than a professional. She owned Shadetree, a prestigious Type A facility for senior adults, after working here for nearly two decades, then investing her husband's life insurance money to buy out the previous owners. She'd become a competent business woman, and while she maintained the position of director, she was far more than that. Forty years had wiped away any connection between her and this indomitable man, so there was nothing for her to get worked up about.

That didn't stop all rational thoughts from careening from her head and shattering her morning into a thousand bone-jarring pieces, as she was taken aback by his response. His penetrating blue eyes locked on hers, he ignored her hand, and he murmured a softly-spoken question, surely intended just for her.

"Is that how you greet an old friend?"

— Earlier That Day —

Beth pulled her car into her officially marked parking space in front of the Center. Director, the sign said. It even reflected her name, Beth Taylor. *Owner*, she thought proudly. Dawn was barely breaking through the trees, and it promised to be a beautiful morning, although the temperatures would soar in the afternoon. It was to be expected on a Texas summer day.

She looked for her young assistant's car. Chloe Owens was wonderful to work with, but some days she was a bit of a panic waiting to happen, and Beth had been out of town for two days. The Department of Aging and Disability Services, known in the industry as DADS, had demanded her attention, and she'd been happy to attend and review the newest policies and procedures for licensing new facilities.

She wondered what Chloe would be panicked over this time. A missing bedside table? An air conditioner on the fritz? At times, it was like the little boy who cried wolf, and Beth the huntress who came to his rescue. She imagined smoothing the feathers of a panicked parakeet who'd never been out of its cage.

She killed the engine and dropped her key fob into her purse before she stepped out of her Cadillac to luxuriate in the heady aroma of the Center's bedding plants in full bloom. They lined the staff parking area, infusing the shade under the massive, lumbering oak trees with cheerful shots of brilliant color. Dew sparkled on the grass, and a spider web glistened in a low boxwood shrub just to her left. Everything was fresh and new, with no hint of the life-altering change that would soon collide with her day. She even looked forward to catching up on all the calls she'd missed.

She walked briskly toward the front door, and with an inward smile, she grasped the door handle, tripping the latch and swinging it wide. She would postpone any changes to the sign at her parking space to another day. Her young secretary had sent her a text that a new resident was arriving this morning, sight unseen; not just coming for a walk-through, but moving in, personal items and all.

That had surprised Beth, but she'd told Chloe she would arrive early to ensure the move went smoothly. Chloe had thanked her profusely in a text ending in a smiley face emoji. The normal procedure was to schedule a meeting, with Beth in attendance when possible, go over the legalities of the contracts, and speak very briefly about payment methods. Then would come the tour of the facilities, of which Beth was extremely proud. Walking prospective residents through the upscale, Type A facility was a favorite activity for her. She would give her facility a superior rating to anyone who asked. It had all the best amenities. She had lovingly decorated the hallways with armoires and bombe chests from local antique shops. Each room had a reading nook with a Queen Anne wingback chair and a Stifle brass lamp. Her favorite feature was the flat-panel television cunningly disguised behind a wall-hanging screen. A touch of a remote, and the television was there in all its gleaming glory. Another touch, and the elegance Beth insisted on in each room reappeared once again.

Beth was fully prepared for her new arrival, and she'd tentatively selected a suite for today's guest. Now to locate her attendant and get things prepared, so there would be no holdups. First would be to ensure the unit was freshened and the bath freshly cleaned.

"Chloe!" Beth breezed into the building, calling her assistant's name, as the soft whoosh of the glass door closing on its pneumatics somehow comforted her. The sound spoke of a facility that was well-oiled, polished, and of the highest caliber. Beth insisted on perfection, and she would allow nothing less. After a moment with no response, she frowned, calling out again, "Chloe, where have you gotten to?"

"Oh, Beth!" Chloe rushed through the grand foyer of the Living Center, dropping several file folders onto a polished mahogany sideboard. Her knee-length linen skirt in pale cream contrasted with her lemon-yellow ruffled blouse underneath her soft green jacket. Her honey-colored hair curled in tendrils and was held by a clip at the nape of her neck. Her nails reflected the color of her blouse, giving her a finished professionalism. It was the pen she pulled from behind one ear and placed soundly on the stack that revealed her chaotic approach to her work.

"About that new arrival. I think Suite 134—" Beth was startled when Chloe cut her off.

"First, let me tell you how my morning's gone. I'm so glad you're here. Why—"

"Slow down!" Beth insisted. Chloe always ran at

the speed of a runaway freight train, and Beth hadn't even had her first cup of coffee. "Remember the text you sent me this morning? We should make this decision now. Unit 134 has a private courtyard with that wonderful oak—"

"I agree, but I've got something more important you'll be interested in." Chloe interrupted again, picking up her pen and tapping it on the folders. "See this stack of folders? If you knew what I've gone through for you—"

"Hold that thought, Chloe," Beth interrupted, reaching a slender, elegant hand to place it on the younger woman's wrist. "First, I need an explanation. That new guest coming in today, you said something about my past catching up with me. Before we move any further through this morning, and certainly before our new guest arrives, I want to know this: What do you know about my past? Really, now, what could possibly be catching up with me?"

Widowed for nearly three years, Beth felt positive she had no history worthy of anyone's notice, certainly nothing that could catch up with her. Her husband was gone after a painful but mercifully brief bout of heart trouble, giving him time to sort his affairs and tell his family goodbye, and leaving her with over three decades of fond memories that only brought back warm times. Robert had attended the Methodist church each Sunday, even taught a Sunday school class for two decades, done nothing questionable his entire life, and their marriage, while not that of storybook dreams, had been a series of carefully orchestrated events, tied together like a string of pearls, if not ones that Beth might have chosen. It was what Robert had been good at, organizing life in a way that removed all the rough edges. Her daughters, well, she loved them, but they weren't extraordinary in any manner that could haunt her. The youngest was like Robert, charming, with not a rough edge in sight. Her eldest, Candy, was a spitfire that loved life, and she loved people to enjoy it with her, building long-lasting friendships with people across all walks of life. They had attended church camps each summer, taken a mission trip or two, and were members of their local fellowships. Candy had counseled at Camp Whispering Trees in Florida just out of college. Her grandchildren? She didn't have any of those, meaning there wasn't a trouble maker among them.

She had no past to catch up with her, not from the past forty years, anyway. It was only when Chloe looked her directly in the eyes that she realized her assistant was still talking to her.

"Beth, that's what I'm trying to tell you." Chloe took her boss's hand, bringing her back to the moment, and she blurted, "You know Lily Pearl Cadence, don't you? For years she lived on that big ranch just out of town. Well, her son called while you were gone, and I've got all the information here in these folders. She's ninety-two years old, no longer able to live alone, and she refuses to be a burden to her son. She just up and decided to check herself in. I tried to tell her you'd prefer to schedule an appointment to show her around. She wouldn't hear of it, told me she wouldn't think of waiting. She's bringing out a check for the first month today. When I tried to explain that a check isn't necessary, she said she knows of our guest policy, and she isn't moving in on anyone's dime. She has money, and she can pay her own way. Luckily, she can't make it until ten this morning. I've been running myself ragged since seven trying to clear out a suite in the new wing. I forgot the remodeling was finished in 134." Chloe sighed, the sound filled with the worries of the world. Her expression changed, and she smiled brightly. "She wants to bring her own furniture, and it will fill one of the largest suites we have, so 134 will be perfect. I guess that's why you're the boss. You think of everything."

"Now if we can just get those final rooms filled." Beth smiled with forced brightness at Chloe's compliment. "What did you say the new resident's last name was?"

A slow, sinking feeling had begun to blur Beth's world, and she reached to take the top folder off the stack. She'd heard the name just fine, and she knew what she was doing. She was putting off facing the reality of the moment. She was on a roller coaster beginning its rapid descent, and she had no control. All she wanted to do was scream. She now thought she should have returned Maggie Jackson's garbled voicemail. Her best friend's message had shown up on her phone during the conference, and Beth had been too preoccupied to get back to her. Poorly transcribed by her smart phone, it had suggested something about old times coming round again.

Then to get a similar message that morning from Chloe? She closed the folder without reading what was inside. What she really needed was a moment to adjust to her disbelief. The Cadence name unlocked the storage bins of her mind, dragging out old, well-worn baggage, and allowing thoughts long suppressed to rise to the surface. Candy, oh, poor Candy. She hoped this wasn't about her lovely daughter. The possible consequences of Lily Pearl in this facility didn't bode well for Beth's peace of mind.

Chloe pulled back the cover of the top file, glanced inside, and she paused. Then, her eyes searching, she stopped and spoke very clearly, "Cadence, capital C-a-d-e-n-c-e. That's her son's name, too."

"Cadence." The phone rang, and Beth took a deep breath as she moved toward her office and sat at her mahogany desk. She picked up the handset, and before she answered it, she covered the receiver with her hand, glanced at Chloe, and murmured, "I know how the name's spelled."

She'd also caught the part about the son, and her heart beat faster with dread, or at least that's what she wanted to believe. No other explanation could be possible for the emotions she was experiencing. There could be only one Lily Pearl Cadence. Beth had known her son quite well, although the connection between them was decades in disuse.

Just minutes into her conversation, Chloe stepped back into the room, whispering, "Oh, Beth, wait a minute. I have one more file in my office. Be right back."

Chloe exited, and through the bank of windows separating the two offices, Beth watched her snatch one from the filing cabinet behind her desk. She returned, holding it out.

"Here!"

The bell from the front door dinged, and Beth covered the phone and called out, "Welcome to Shadetree Assisted Living Center." Then she reached for the file, while smiling brightly and trying desperately to cover her troubled feelings. "Do these folders by any chance say who the son is?"

Again, she was putting off what she already knew, wanting to put as much distance between the past and the present as she could. Despite her efforts, her heart turned over just asking the question.

"Maverick, capital M-a-v-e-r-i-c-k."

A man's deep voice spoke the words, and Beth looked up in dismay. At the sight of the visitor in the foyer, her heart truly turned over, leaving her emotions in a puddle. She gripped the phone in her hand and knew she couldn't maintain a proper conversation to the person on the other end in the light of who had walked in the Center's door.

"Thank you. I'll call back later." Beth spoke the words carefully into the mouthpiece and drew in a deep breath. She dropped the phone into its cradle, slowly and without conscious thought. Cascading ribbons of memories flashed in front of her eyes, few of them welcome. She felt the last forty years of her life evaporate, forty years of perfect children, an equally successful marriage, and a social life that was the envy of half the county. She narrowed her eyes at the tall, silver-headed gentleman in starched blue jeans. A crisp white shirt under a leather blazer complemented his tanned skin. It was the same face she remembered from four decades before. His piercing blue eyes completed her devastation, with the same steely glint he had wowed her with years ago.

She could not have this man here in her life, not now, not ever. There was no room for him under the scar he'd put on her heart. He had run away, and he should have stayed away.

"Maverick?" Beth barely managed her shattered reply. Her voice sounded hollow and shaky to her ears. She felt helpless. Maverick had always done this to her, made her soft and weak, and it was happening again. Unable to respond rationally, she simply stood and reached out one hand.

"Is that how you greet an old friend?" murmured his resonating voice.

"An old friend?" Chloe's eyes danced between the two.

Before Beth could manage to think through this disastrous moment, she felt Maverick's strong arms pull her off her feet. Her intruding ghost from the past picked her up in a bear-like hug, holding her in an embrace that was a little too long for her to feel comfortable.

"Well, Marilyn, how are you?" Maverick's strong, slow, baritone drawl pulled at her heart. He set her down, and his eyes studied her face, evaluating her. "You look great, and, if you'll allow me to say so without running away to hide, you smell good, too. My word, girl, you're just like I remember from high school."

"High school? What could you possibly remember from all those years ago? I've forgotten so much that I'm surprised I even recognize you."

Beth's lips quivered slightly as she finished the sarcastic words, and she hoped she sounded convincing. She wanted to appreciate his effusive compliments, but a strong undercurrent of irritation in the back of her mind dashed all that like a Texas soaker on a hot summer afternoon. Maverick's comments sent her thoughts reeling through a succession of memories, most pushed aside for more decades than she wished to recount. Her final two years in high school had been the most special of her life, and she had felt beautiful. Then, Maverick had turned her existence into a living nightmare.

She was sure her dismissal of his unnecessary references to a time better forgotten would distance this man from her life. If she claimed she hadn't recognized him, he'd know she'd forgotten all about him. He would see that he was an intrusion into her well-ordered life, and he would wrap up his business with his mother quickly and efficiently, exiting the premises as quickly as possible.

Then Beth's secret and heart would be safe once again.

MAVERICK'S EYES SPARKLED, and his face brightened. He chuckled as he began to speak.

"If you don't recognize me, that must mean I've either gotten better looking or just the opposite. I don't know which I'll claim. You've hardly changed at all. You still have that fabulous blonde hair; it's just not in a shag anymore. I like it down like it is now. It reminds me of your senior picture."

His heart cinched tightly in his chest, as long-forgotten emotions tumbled through his veins. He took a deep breath, aware of the past like a journal that had recorded every event from their relationship, and the pages were peeling themselves away, faster and faster. He hadn't expected this strong of a response. He had been looking forward to staying for the upcoming reunion the following week, but now? He needed to change the subject fast before this woman pushed him to the point of no return.

"MY SENIOR PICTURE?" Beth barely got out the words, but she was determined to control her reaction and not reveal what she truly thought. She couldn't reveal how he'd crushed and bruised her heart all those years ago. Her sweet husband Robert had been her only salvation, rescuing her from the morass this man had strewn across her world. For years, with Robert as her guide, she'd successfully entertained her husband's clients, hosting fabulous parties for the moneyed investment bankers who had been Robert's business associates. Now, alone, she ran this assisted living facility, and very successfully, too. How could she be falling apart in front of this man? She hadn't known this melting feeling inside for four decades, not since the last occasion she'd spent time with him.

She felt her jaw tighten with determination, refusing to reveal any weakness. Her assistant gave a little cough, causing Beth to warm with the thickly layered praise.

"I go by Beth, now, Maverick," Beth whispered, biting her lip. She kicked herself for calling his given name. She knew she must keep this formal, otherwise, who knew where things would wind up? Self-consciously, she adjusted her rose-colored blouse and dark skirt and attempted to make light of the moment.

"I'm glad your looks haven't changed." He winked at her. "A woman as beautiful as you should have the best parking space in the lot, which I see you've taken."

With a flip of her hand in her hair and a bright bravado to her voice, Beth quipped, "It's just that now my blonde gets a little help from a bottle."

She hardly felt as effusive as she hoped she sounded. This morning had fled from her control, and she didn't know how she would get it back.

"A genie from a bottle?" Maverick chuckled.

"I did not say that!" Beth glanced at Chloe, hoping for some help. Instead, her assistant was covering a smile of her own with one hand.

"I'm sorry for laughing, but you'll have to speak up a little, Marilyn. Phnom Penh got some of my hearing." Maverick paused, waiting on Beth.

"No one calls me Marilyn, anymore," Beth repeated louder. She wasn't sure if she felt irritation or relief at having to repeat the words. She knew one thing: Maverick wouldn't be allowed a toehold back into her life.

His next words shook her resolve.

"No? Well, that's a shame with those good looks and all." Humor laced the words, and the big man grinned again as he watched Beth.

Beth felt her face warm as she closed her eyes and stifled a groan. She cleared her throat, determined to ask about his mother. That's why he'd come, and getting back to business was her only hope now. A dozen words from that man's mouth, and her knees felt about to buckle.

Maverick leaned over Chloe's desk and winked at the young assistant standing just behind. "You'd think a woman would enjoy being Marilyn Monroe, wouldn't you? Ours may have been a little thinner, but she certainly looked like a movie star. Well, as far as I can tell, she still does."

"Maverick!" It was hopeless. Beth was convinced her face had turned deep red. She certainly felt the warmth of embarrassment. And to have told such a thing to Chloe! Even so, she remembered those years, and how it had secretly given her a certain amount of pleasure to be compared to the blonde beauty from the heyday of the big screen. She cringed at what Maverick shared next.

"But not this one," he pointed to Beth. "She always said her name was Mary Elizabeth Monroe anytime we tried to tease her about it. Isn't that right, Marilyn?"

"Yes. I wanted to be liked for who I was and not the person someone else wanted me to be."

What Beth wanted to scream was, *Stop talking about all this!* How could she fend off this man if he continued to say things to remind her of how much she had loved him all those years ago . . . no! Not loved! She couldn't have loved him. No, their relationship had been a mistake, and she wouldn't let go of that thought. She had been a youthful, idealistic girl, and he'd abandoned her, shattering her dreams. This man would not charm his way into her affections, um, under her skin ever again.

Only the sound of the carts carrying the midmorning brunch trays shifted Beth's thoughts back to the moment. She tamped down her emotions. These were her surroundings, her office. Maverick was in her place. She put a stern look on her face to make sure there was no question how she felt.

MAVERICK'S WORDS WERE a compliment he'd

waited with bated breath to deliver. After all, he'd held on for forty years to make its delivery, and he intended to enjoy this moment to the fullest. He had no trouble reading the nuance of Beth's every expression. He was quite aware this could only be her space. It looked like her. He'd taken in the spacious surroundings, missing nothing, including the small silver-framed photos sitting pristinely on Beth's expansive, hand-carved Chippendale desk. This was an opulent facility, just the sort of environment she'd grown up with. He wasn't surprised by the expensive taste he observed everywhere.

The phone rang, and Chloe picked it up. After a moment, she held it out to Beth, calling, "It's for you, Mrs. Taylor."

Beth picked up the phone and stepped aside for a moment, answering a few questions from the caller. She glanced at Maverick several times, pausing once as if she intended to ask him to come to the phone. By that time, he'd struck up a conservation with Chloe.

"Tell me again Marilyn's last name." He could barely keep the grin from his face. This was a doozy.

"Taylor, but she truly goes by Beth. I've never heard her called Marilyn. She was an actress, right? I've never watched old movies much."

"Taylor, like Elizabeth?"

"Yes, like the movie star. She was in *Lassie*, I think. I watched it some as a girl."

"That and a few others." Maverick began to laugh, thinking that there were about seventy-five more. When Beth hung up, she turned and looked at Maverick with a frown. That caused him to laugh even more.

BETH STARTED TO CALL to him, then the thought hit her, she had pulled up in the best parking space in the lot? How did he know where she parked? Had he been outside all along watching her? It was something he had done all those years ago, telling her he couldn't get of enough of her. She had found it flattering then. Now? She refused to admit his gratuitous words still affected her, even made her knees feel weak.

"Okay, Mr. Cadence. What's so funny?" Beth punched out his name, the snap in her voice bracing her determination. She took a deep breath, steadying herself. She would need to speak carefully to keep this situation under control.

"Your name is now Elizabeth Taylor? So, Marilyn Monroe wasn't good enough for you?" His eyes crinkled, and he placed one hand on his stomach as he shook with laughter. At his side, Chloe wasn't helping. She was laughing, also.

Beth looked pointedly at her assistant, immediately subduing Chloe's laughter. Then she turned to Maverick. "My late husband was Robert Alexander Taylor. I still go by my married name. I volunteered here when he was still alive, and all my residents have come to know me by that name. I see no reason to change it now."

The words briefly weighed on her. Speaking of Robert made her miss his companionship even three years after his death. She guessed what everyone told her was true. A part of her would probably always miss him.

Then she remembered the phone call.

"That was your mother calling to say she'll be late, but the moving van is on the way. She's made an appointment to get her hair done, and the hairdresser is running behind. She refuses to be seen in her new home without looking her best. She gave me strict instructions to tell Maverick to take the tour in her stead."

"She did, huh?" The laughter was still in his voice, and he turned to Chloe and gave an exaggerated wink. "Sounds as if it's better for her to be here with you two than in her townhouse or out on the ranch with me. She's wearing herself out corralling both her in-town and ranch staff. Two houses are far too much for her to manage and maintain her active social calendar."

"Maverick!" For the second time, Beth found reason to call the man on his behavior. That was like old times, too. Maverick never had been one to pay too much attention to rules he thought superfluous.

Just like . . . Candy, but Beth pushed that thought away.

She tried to control her tone by being bright with her next words. "Lily sounds as feisty as ever. I'm sure we'll love having her with us. She'll keep us on our toes."

Beth remembered Maverick's mother from when they were in high school. Maverick had been a couple of years older than Beth, but they'd gone to many of the same functions, even to his house with the sports crowd a time or two after football games. Lily was everyone's mother, having kids over to support the team. She was also one to stick her finger in everyone's pie. Somehow Beth seemed to always get paired up with Maverick at Lily's extra-curricular activities.

"Feisty? That and more. After Dad's death three-and-a-half years ago, well, I guess it tripped something in Mom. And now, she's worse." The humor in Maverick's words was gone. His voice sounded dry and empty, bringing a pang of sympathy from deep within Beth. This was clearly a painful topic for him.

"I'm so sorry to hear about that. I remember seeing the news. We'll certain do our best for Lily. Is there anything else we need to know?" Beth could hear the unexpected tiredness in his voice, and tender emotions welled up in her.

"Even when I tell you, you won't believe me. Mom went on a selling spree. You remember how she always collected everything. Toward the end of Dad's life, it almost became hoarding. Suddenly, she attempted to liquidate everything. Well, almost. She still has most of her antique furniture and some of her collectables, but the farm implements and other equipment? Gone. Dad's Model T wasn't even spared. She tried to parcel out the ranch, saying she wanted to live in town for her final years. She'd already sold off twelve hundred acres before I found out, so I told her I'd buy the rest from her. We argued for weeks, but at least she didn't sell the remaining eighteen hundred. I managed to save part of my family heritage and the history that goes with it, but you can't run a whole lot of cattle on that. I don't know what I'll do with it eventually, but that's neither here nor there at this point. For the past three years, she's been living in town. Finally, I've forced her to admit that it's just too much. When I found out some months ago that you were the administrator of this place, it was like an answer to prayer."

That shot Beth's astonishment meter off the charts. She was an answer to prayer for Maverick? Since when did Maverick pray, ever? And for her? Even though her family went faithfully, she didn't remember Maverick ever going to church. This was one more reason to steer clear of this tangled hunk of walking trouble, no matter what her heart told her.

She attempted to steer the conversation onto a more neutral track.

"Everyone says that, Mr. Cadence. The general consensus of our residents and their families is that Shadetree Assisted Living Center is certainly an answer to prayer." Beth caught Chloe's puzzled look, frowning sharply when her assistant mouthed silently, *They say what?* Ignoring Chloe's question, Beth smiled forcefully at Maverick, determined to maintain control of this situation.

"Is there anything I need to do as far as paperwork before Mom moves in? If not, then I want that tour my mom said I should take."

"Paperwork you asked for, and paperwork you shall have, Mr. Cadence. Chloe?" Beth motioned for her assistant to get on the ball. She was feeling his charm, er, his overpowering, um, overbearing assumptions making her nervous. It was Chloe's turn to pick up the slack.

Chloe efficiently handed him a packet. She smiled as she spoke, "This is everything you'll need to fill out before she takes occupancy. Some of the forms will need to be notarized, but we can do that right here. In addition to being Mrs. Taylor's personal assistant, I'm a legally qualified notary."

"Ah! I'm not to be allowed to forget that there are *two* beautiful people in the room." He turned to Chloe and took the packet. He thanked her and kissed her hand, causing the young woman to blush with pleasure. "I'm sure we'll be seeing more of each other."

With those words Beth remembered what she hadn't liked about Maverick all those years ago: his flirting. She could never tell when he was serious, just like now. That was the part that had unnerved her around him then, and it was clear he hadn't changed a bit. Her late husband hadn't been that way at all. He was a considerate man and a stable father to her two daughters. He would sometimes push Beth to do more than she wanted, but that was only due to her natural shyness. He always said it was for her own good, and look how she'd put all that aside, entertaining for her husband over decades, and now running the Center. Thank God for Robert. With him, she had always known where she stood. His consistency had made her feel safe and secure.

Maverick would have never given her safe and secure. He bordered on reckless. Driving too fast, taking too many chances, like signing up for military service, then going off to war. He didn't have to enlist. There was college, the fact that he was an only child, and his parents owned a ranch where he was needed. It had surprised Beth that his father and mother didn't even try to stop him. At least he was one of the lucky ones who came back. Even then he didn't stay long, only a few weeks. As fast as he could get his boots shined, he moved away.

Beth heard he later married and had a son and a daughter. Now here he was, drawn back once more to his old home, checking on his mother.

At least no one could say he wasn't a good son.

"Well, how about it?"

The words interrupted Beth's thoughts, jerking her back to the present.

"What? I'm sorry. I wasn't listening. What did you ask?" She'd tried to rise above Maverick, presenting a very business-like approach in her dealings with him. Now she felt embarrassed. She had no idea he'd been speaking to her.

"Are you going to give me the nickel tour, or do I

have to get your pretty little secretary to help me?"

At her assistant's eager expression, Beth brightly called out, "Chloe, can you show Mr. Cadence around?"

"Of course, Mrs. Taylor."

"Chloe can answer most of your questions, I'm sure. Please have a good morning, Mr. Cadence."

With that, Chloe excitedly got up from her desk and put her arm through Maverick's extended one. "Now, this is the main lobby," she began, as she walked him toward the spacious foyer. Pointing to the back of the building, she noted one of the establishment's most elegant amenities. "We even have a Steinway grand, permanently donated to our facility by a resident's family."

The tour disappeared down a hallway toward the new wing. Beth felt like a rag doll long due for a refit. She knew what had done it: meeting Maverick again after four decades. She'd certainly never expected that. If she'd been forced to give him the tour, she wouldn't have survived. Of all things, that man putting his mother here!

It was only a little after ten, and Beth realized she was done for the day. Today Maverick had caught her off guard. She might be forced to deal with him because of his mother, but she would be more prepared in the future. This wouldn't happen again.

She arched her back as she ran her fingers through her thick hair, pushing it away from her face, while trying to ward off an impending headache. Home sounded good. Chloe could corral the residents the rest of the day.

WHAT BETH DIDN'T NOTICE was the silhouette she revealed through her glass office wall. Chloe had forgotten the key to the new wing, and Maverick was waiting in the foyer. He had a very clear view of Beth as she stretched to ease the pain.

"I'm back, Beth," he whispered to no one in particular. "This time I won't run away. I can promise you that."

It was eight days until the reunion, he had already set his trap, and now he had to sit back and wait for it to spring.

— 2 —

THE PHONE JANGLED, shattering the silence of the night, before going quiet. Beth flung her comforter to the side, squinting at the windows stretching across the back wall of her bedroom. She was surprised to see sunlight already peeking in through the plantation shutters. She worked her hands over her face, starting at her eyes, and letting her fingers make their way to her temples.

"I told the decorator my east-facing windows needed light-blocking drapes, not shutters," she moaned. The phone jangled again, and she winced. "My word! Who could be calling me this early in the morning?"

She recalled the sermon last Sunday titled, "Don't Hold Back." The theme had been based on music and how Christians should let the love of Christ be a song in their hearts. She glared at the phone, thinking that if they could just remaster phones to ring in your heart to wake you up gently, that would be fine with her.

When she rolled over and looked at the clock, the time jarred her awake. It was nearly eight. There would be no time for her regular run, nor for her accustomed after-run morning shower. Maggie would have to understand when she skipped breakfast, too. She'd be good to get her face on and out the door by nine. She laid the blame squarely where it belonged, on Maverick. He'd shown back up in her life, and that had her rattled. She tossed and turned until she'd given in and taken a sleeping aid.

Now look where it had gotten her.

When the phone jangled again, she lifted the receiver and placed it to her ear.

"Yes?" She half expected Maverick's gravelly voice, or at least Lily Pearl's. If it was either of those two, she could claim two ruined days in a row.

The response over the line was even worse than she expected.

"Ready, Miss Morning Sunshine?" It was Maggie, and she giggled at her brilliance. "I'm sorry I'm running late, but you know me. How was your jog this morning? I bet you've been five miles, and you're on your exercise bike just waiting on Little Miss Come Lately to show. I had to repair a chipped nail, but I'll be there in ten."

Even though they were the same age, Maggie still had a child-like quality about life. Nothing ruffled her feathers. From cars to shoes, she kept them until they went out of style, or they didn't feel right anymore. The only thing she'd held onto for more than a decade had been her friendship with Beth.

Right then, Beth wasn't so sure *that* was going to survive much longer.

"Maggie, dear, I'm hanging up now. Yesterday was atrocious, and I just can't be friends with you or anyone at this moment. The fact is I overslept, and I need to shower before I go anywhere. Let's make it another day, okay?" Beth felt the memory of Maverick wash over her, and the very thought filled her with looming frustration.

She didn't get a peaceful response, as much as she wanted to wish the world away.

"Absolutely not! You've put me off long enough. Hurry and grab a shower, and I'll meet you at Deep South's for breakfast. I'll have your coffee ready for you. Now, hurry up!" There was a suppressed giggle, and the phone went dead.

What could be so important that Maggie couldn't let her get a few more minutes of sleep, anyway? Beth tiredly sat up in bed. The phone in her hand wasn't in the mood to give her that answer, though, and Beth was in no frame of mind to call Maggie back.

At least it was Friday, and the workweek was almost over.

Knowing it would help force her awake, she hit the button on her bedside table to trigger the shutters. With a gentle whirring noise, the slats rolled around, sending brilliant sunshine arcing into the room. She squinted, but it was working. She would never find sleep again after that wakeup shock.

It was in her closet that she remembered the casual Friday rule she'd let Chloe talk her into several months back. Casual Friday, she considered, touching several of her most easy-going dresses. Then her finger touched one she'd almost forgotten about. Maggie had talked her into it a couple months ago during a trip to the outlet mall, and she had given in because it was on sale.

She hadn't worn it, even once.

There had been no occasion in her leisure time, and it was just a bit more vibrant than she normally wore to work. But Maverick! He had her remembering her high school years—not that it was a good thing—and the soft, raspberry sherbet dress called to her. Besides, it was almost summer, with the temperature predicted to be in the 90s. This along with some casual heels, and she could carry a light jacket for indoors. The dress would be very presentable no matter that it left her shoulders completely exposed, and anyway, the color was perfect.

Her lipstick wasn't.

When she opened the lid, she remembered she'd meant to stop and pick up some at the mall on her way home yesterday. Then her past had crashed into her day, and exhaustion had careened her into every obstacle that could possibly beset her. The mall had flown from her thoughts, and marshmallow rose was empty.

"Thank you, Candy!" Beth reached for the golden tube she could just see hiding in the back of the drawer. Her elder daughter had bought it for her the previous Christmas, telling her it was to brighten her holiday. It had been bright enough that Beth hadn't touched it since. Despite that, it was quality, and she hadn't been able to bring herself to throw it away. Now she was glad she hadn't, as she couldn't go out without lipstick.

This, though, would have to be dabbed lightly.

It was easier said than done. Trust her daughter to buy only the best. One touch, no matter how gingerly applied, was as good as a fierce stroke of her regular lipstick. Beth made a face, and then she laughed. Her eyes! Where had they gone? Her normal brown mascara was a faded flower against her newly brilliant lips.

She glanced at the clock. There was no time to remove the deep crimson. Knowing just what to do, she reached into her closet and rummaged in a drawer. She had a tube of black mascara from an evening social several weeks before. Pulling the brush free, she nodded, satisfied. This would be the perfect foil for the brilliance she'd inadvertently painted across her lips.

She leaned into the mirror, and with a flick of her

fingers and a blink into the brush, she stepped back and tried to see herself in the best light possible.

"Lands! I could see this face if there was no light at all. I'm a walking Christmas tree!"

This was makeup for candle-lit dinners and walks in the dark, not for breakfast in the brilliance of a summer morning. She closed the mascara tube and tossed it carelessly on the counter. It was just Maggie she was meeting. Her friend would laugh at her lipstick, Beth would let her excuses dance around the table, and it would be good for a joke for the next month or so. See? she told herself. You're waking up, after all. Opening those blinds was the perfect way to get that sleeping pill out of your system.

"Breakfast, here I come! Maggie, girl, ready or not, you're in for a shock!"

Giving in to the inevitable, Beth headed out of her bathroom and grabbed her key fob. She hoped the long-wearing 18-hour lipstick would somehow lessen and wear off during breakfast.

It had better. She would be embarrassed to wear it all day.

"WELL, MAGGIE D, I see your Mini, and I see an empty space right next to it. Thank the Lord for that."

Beth was at the signal light, waiting to turn into the parking lot, with her blinker clicking off the seconds. A strip of grass accented by small shrubs bordered the street, and closer to the stone, glass, and metal-roofed building, park benches lined the sidewalk for those who needed a place to wait during the restaurant's busy times. It wasn't unusual to have a twenty-minute line around lunchtime. This morning, the parking lot had plenty of empty spaces, but most of them were in the north forty and nowhere near the shade. With the Texas heat warming up early this spring, a cool spot to park her vehicle was highly coveted. The light glinting on the window of her friend's Mini Cooper suggested a lighthearted playfulness that went right along with its owner, but Beth wasn't in a playful mood.

"Maggie, you'd better have my coffee waiting, because my stomach was growling three lights ago." Beth muttered the words as she swung the long hood of her big Cadillac into the empty space, stopping when her parking sensors screamed at her that enough was enough. One look in the mirror telling her that she was barely inside the line filled her with relief that she'd listened to Maggie when selecting this latest Cadillac. Beth had wanted a new SUV, and Maggie had cautioned her about buying something so large. Now Beth was glad to have a smaller vehicle, even if it was the largest sedan the company made. It barely fit in this space.

Walking up to the glass door, her reflection revealed her care at putting herself together. She smiled as she tucked her hair behind one ear, pleased with how soft it felt. Stepping inside, she was less pleased. The space was bright and open, but the wood floors didn't muffle the kitchen sounds or the chattering voices from the various diners. Something with dim lights and thick carpeting would have been a nice choice, and she began to wish she hadn't listened to her friend when she'd suggested Deep South's. She could do this, though, and she put a bright expression on her face as she looked for Maggie.

Beth's smile froze on her lips. She shook her head as she stared and blinked slowly, making sure her vision was clear. Of all things, Maverick was here, and she didn't see how she would avoid him, as he sat in the same booth with her friend! Her panic rising, she glanced around to see what other options were available. A table, perhaps, or she could request they sit at the counter. Maybe she could bypass them on her way to the restroom and continue out the back door. She didn't even have to stay for breakfast. Maggie and Maverick had each other for company, and they'd do fine on their own.

Then Maggie waved at her, and Beth knew she wasn't to be allowed out of this. When she stepped up to the booth, Maverick's Stetson and Maggie's over-sized purse were next to Maggie, conveniently filling a good portion of the seat. Beth hesitated, wanting to ask if she could move the items, and realizing in the same thought how rude that would sound.

"Hey, there. Good morning, Beth. Hand me your purse, and I'll put it with mine. It'll give you more room on your side of the booth."

Beth had no desire to be rude, and her friend's request left her no choice but to offer to slide in next to

Maverick. However, she didn't have to like it.

"Good morning, Mags," Beth mumbled, barely keeping the words coherent. There were three cups of coffee already on the table, one on Maggie's side, and two on the opposite. Beth had yet to look at Maverick. She shot her friend a look of fire before glancing at her seat. She told herself that she had to check to make sure the bench was clear. Some men put their sunglasses or wallet beside them. Good manners. In nice restaurants, one never put keys or other personal items on the dining table.

As she shifted her gaze, her eyes swept over Maverick's bulk, his shoulders hunched over the table, and his hands encircling his cup. In that glance, she knew this morning would come to no good. Good had been the security Robert had provided. Good was a new resident checking into the Center, assuring all the bills were paid and sweet Chloe had a steady paycheck. Good was knowing that the man at your side would promise a relationship and then follow through, rather than running off to a war on the other side of the world. Good was not feeling that the previous four decades had never happened, and that despite all the warning bells in her head, she still fit at this man's side like a hand in a glove.

Beth knew one thing for certain: What had gone on in high school should stay in high school.

No forty-year-dead relationship would be allowed to shake up her life now. She would see to that. A properly phrased rebuttal would set Maverick on his ear. She had promised Maggie she would meet her for breakfast, so she might not be able to turn and walk out the door, without feeling like he had made her leave, but this man would know where she stood before breakfast was over.

As Beth reached for a copy of the menu, her hand shook with emotions she thought long forgotten. She remembered how angry she'd been when Maverick had burned the bridges between them all those decades ago. She'd loved him at one time, but the hurt and anger had long eclipsed that. She refused to admit that her flushed skin and beating heart felt distinctly the same as before Maverick had destroyed every connection they'd ever built between them, and she let her irritation continue to grow. Her carefully phrased retort would have a bite to it when she figured out just what to say.

His next words shattered all that.

"Hmm. You smell good again today. How are you, Marilyn?" He reached to slip the quavering menu from her fingers, and he opened it to the inside, just as he used to do all those years ago. One beefy finger pointed to the section at the bottom of the page. "Just there, Marilyn. Order anything you want. The tab's mine."

Beth glanced at him as he spoke, seeing the old ways his expression danced with his words. He'd been exactly this way at seventeen, taking control smoothly and with no effort at all. She also noticed when he glanced at Maggie, and something passed between them. What, Beth couldn't tell. Not romance, surely! A joke they'd shared before she arrived?

Anyway, it didn't matter. All she needed was time and the opportunity to come up with a sharp retort, and he and Maggie could joke all morning long. For now, she intended to focus on the menu in peace and quiet, without being involved in any bantering conversation. It irritated her Maverick had assumed she wouldn't be able to find the breakfast section on the menu. This wasn't her first time up to bat, or to order from a restaurant menu.

"Beth," Maggie broke the silence, speaking softly and tentatively, "I told you your past was coming back to haunt you, but you didn't call me back to find more."

"Call you back?" Beth looked at her hard, throwing out her words like a brick tossed into a bucket of mouse traps.

"Yes, on the phone. Anyway, we can't undo what's been done, so, heeere's your past. It's Maaa-verick!" She giggled, and it was the same one from the phone that morning. She winked, also, although so slightly it was almost nonexistent.

Beth felt her irritation flare.

The waitress walked up, shutting down the conversation. She topped off Maverick's and Maggie's coffee, and she glanced at Beth. "Honey, you haven't touched a drop in that cup. That coffee's going to get cold pretty soon. I just made a fresh batch. Would you like to start over?"

Beth smiled and wrapped both hands around her cup, and it began to quiver in her fingers. She didn't guess she'd calmed down that much. Taking a sip, she nodded at the waitress.

"It's perfect. I'm fine."

"Okay, honey. You let me know when you want a refresh. Would you like a moment before you order?" She made as if to pull her pad from her apron pocket, hesitating when Beth pursed her lips in thought.

"Thank you. Two minutes, please," Maggie said brightly. "You can wait to bring out our order until then, if you don't mind. We won't starve if my friend can decide. You can decide on a breakfast choice, Beth?" Maggie chuckled, and she winked at Beth.

"Gotcha," the waitress acknowledged. "Be back in two. Gotta get this pot back to the kitchen. Fresh coffee coming up next go round." And she was gone.

Beth didn't bother with the menu. She glared at Maggie. If she'd known Maverick would be here at breakfast, she'd have driven straight to the Center. She could have caught the end of breakfast there, and that would have suited her fine. The center served meals of the highest quality, and she felt honored to dine in the establishment she owned anytime the opportunity provided itself.

With that thought, casual Friday leaped into her mind. Dear jumping jelly beans! This dress! She'd left the jacket in the car. And heaven forbid, she had on Candy's lipstick!

Her heart sank. She pictured her mascara; it was

just as bold, and totally inappropriate sitting here next to this man. She'd thought she was a walking Christmas tree. She wasn't just the Christmas tree, she was Macy's on parade, the whole schlemiel down Fifth Avenue. Her arms tensed with distress. Could this morning get any worse?

"Beth?" Maggie tapped Beth's wrist. "I guess you didn't hear me. Your past? Coming back to haunt you? You do remember Maverick, don't you?" Her eyes twinkled as she spoke.

The woman knew she was pushing old buttons that had long been in disuse, and that wasn't sitting well with Beth. She retorted, very drily, "I saw him yesterday, and you could have told me he was coming." *Should have* was what she wanted to say. As in, over the phone this morning. instead of giggling so rudely and waking her up from a sound sleep.

The thought of what she was wearing was ever-present in her mind. There was no way she could hide it. It leaped off her lips and eyes, screaming from her bare shoulders. Look at me! I'm nothing more than a silly junior high schoolgirl, begging to be noticed!

It helped a bit when Maggie complimented Beth on what she wore, telling her she'd known the dress would look this sweet on her, even when it had been hanging on the rack. It didn't help when Maverick interjected his take on her clothing choices.

"You know, yesterday you were in high CEO mode. I knew I was speaking to the same girl I'd known all those years ago, but I was having trouble finding you through all those Mr. Cadences. Now look at you. This is the pretty thing I knew in high school, only better. Whoa!" He gave a soft whistle.

Beth felt her face warm. She was rescued by the waitress, and she eagerly snatched up the menu, focusing on the pictures on the page.

"Honey, you still have a full cup. Let me replace that in a moment. You don't drink another drop. Coffee cold is nasty as brown water. Now, are you ready to order a bite to eat? A breakfast a day keeps the hunger pangs away." A pop of chewing gum finished the quip.

"Blueberry bagel, please." With Maverick being so close, Beth knew she wouldn't be able to eat. She could nibble, though. That would get her through until lunch, and she could eat at the Center. Veal was on the menu. Veal with baby carrots and apple pie a la mode. Focus, she told herself. Think of lunch. Veal. Baby carrots. Apple pie. A la mode.

"Gotcha, honey. Anyone else? No? Be back with your food right away."

A la mode. Vanilla. Strawberry. Banana nut. Banana shake. Chocolate shake. Pineapple upside down cake. Lunch!

"Is that how you've stayed so skinny all these years, just eating a bagel?" Maverick elbowed her gently.

Beth looked up to see him glance at Maggie and wink. Bagel? This was all about dessert and lunch. Now he was flirting with Maggie? She defended her breakfast choice, and very pointedly. This was her chance to set this man in his place.

"I normally eat a very big breakfast. Veal. Apple pie. A chocolate shake to top it all off. You see, I'm not the girl you used to know. I've changed. I do my own thing now, and I'm very independent. You just mind your manners, Mr. Maverick Cadence." Having burst forth with her unprepared and totally out-of-character tirade, she sagged inside. Had she really said all that? To Maverick? What if he laughed at her? The morning was only getting worse!

"You don't eat all that." Maverick grinned. "You couldn't, not and keep that waistline. Tell me the truth, Marilyn. What's going on?"

"Yeah, Beth. What's going on?" Maggie rustled her keys. She'd had no problem strewing her personal items across the table, and the banter was growing exciting. She could hardly hold her hands still.

Beth's arrogance fled in the light of her embarrassment. The truth fluttered its age-old butterfly wings against her denial. Maverick was at her side, and without understanding just what had been taken from her all those years ago, she'd missed him for most of her life. Robert had been a stalwart stanchion of security and stability, and her kids had been a bright spot she'd always treasure, but Maverick had been her heart and soul.

With Robert gone and her kids away, she was a tumbleweed on the prairie, blown about by her emotions. She sighed, retreating to something safe and normal.

"I didn't sleep well last night. Maybe I'll want something for lunch, but now, no. Coffee and my bagel will be fine. Besides, I'm not that skinny anymore. I fight the extra pounds every day."

Maverick laughed, and it was the boisterous sound Beth remembered, one that boiled up from deep with his chest. "Don't fight those extra pounds so hard. The ones I see are in all the right places."

"Stop teasing her so much, Maverick. You're making her blush." Maggie dropped two extra sugar cubes in her coffee. Her spoon clinked against the ceramic as she tapped it on the side. "I'm so glad they combined half a decade of graduates in our Fortieth Reunion. That'll make it more interesting. With five classes next weekend at the get-together, it'll be amusing trying to guess who people are and see how much some of them have changed. I can't wait to see Buzz. He was so cute when he was a senior; I wonder what he looks like now."

Maggie rambled on brightly about the reunion, nonstop even as the waitress placed their food before them. That was Maggie, though, ever interested in the latest, newest, and best.

Beth was grateful to have something to do with her hands besides hold a hot coffee cup and try to keep it from sloshing out onto the table. She kept catching whiffs of Maverick's cologne. It wasn't the same as in high school, but it suited him, with a deep, woodsy scent, not at all like Robert's sports-type fragrances.

In between bites of her toasted bagel, she learned that Maverick was now widowed as well. She didn't pry. She couldn't. She could barely keep her bagel down, although she would have liked to know everything. *Just for old time's sake*, she told herself. He didn't elaborate, and Maggie refused to ask.

Maverick was more effusive about his children. His son was with the government in the Middle East on a peace-keeping mission, apparently burning with the same wild, reckless ambition as his father. His daughter, adopted by Maverick and his wife as a baby, had been killed by a drunk driver a decade before. At the present he had no grandchildren.

"I bet you two are wondering why I'm eating this strange concoction." Maverick had a pile of food before him, and he shifted two of the plates.

Beth had missed his order, and her eyes hadn't left her bagel. She glanced his way to see turkey sausage, an omelet that was clearly egg white only, and a pile of pancakes. His coffee was black like hers.

"You're hungry?" Maggie quipped. She cut a bite of ham and dipped it in maple syrup before placing it on her tongue. "I thought that's why we gathered in this fine dining establishment for breakfast."

Beth cleared her throat. "Turkey sausage?" At the Center they served it all the time. She knew turkey. That meant something. Maverick had heart issues? Concern gripped her, although she put it off as no more than a general feeling of interest in his health.

At the Center, it was something she dealt with every day.

"You noticed." He grinned appreciatively, picking up a slice and biting off a chunk. "When Dad was diagnosed with heart trouble about twelve years ago, I changed some of my habits."

"Not you, then." Was that relief Beth heard in her voice? She refused to think so.

"Ticker's sound." Maverick tapped his chest. "Just caution. I'm now smoke free, and I've eliminated as much cholesterol and fat from my daily routine as possible. However, there's one thing I haven't given up. Butter." He grinned as he put a large dollop on his pancakes and covered it with maple syrup.

"Oh, that looks good, Maverick." Maggie held her fork poised in the air. "I just thought ham and syrup was the way to go. I should have ordered pancakes. Strawberries. Can you picture that with sliced strawberries dribbled all over? Talk about dying and going to heaven." She licked her lips appreciatively.

"No strawberries, Maggie." Maverick chuckled. He'd already cut off a big chunk, spearing it with his fork. He handed it to Beth. "Try it. You'll like it." He grinned, imitating an old TV commercial, making Maggie giggle.

Beth glared at her old friend. She didn't want to take Maverick's fork, and especially not the fat-laden, rich pancake. Rudeness was not her forte, and she considered how to demurely refuse.

Maverick repeated his request. "Try it, Marilyn.

They really are the best pancakes anywhere. I've lived all over the world, and I'm never satisfied until I come back here. Everything I love is always waiting on me right here in my hometown."

Everything he loves? Pancakes were waiting on him? She couldn't imagine what else he expected to be waiting on him.

"I'm sorry, Maverick, but no." Beth tried to push his hand away.

"But yes." He grinned and refused to back down.

"Just one bite, then, and very small." She took the fork and bit off a portion of the pancake. In that moment, she was reminded of why Deep South's had a reputation for the best pancakes served anywhere in this part of the country. A drop of the syrup ran down her chin, and she lifted her napkin to catch it. Folding the napkin and setting it beside her plate, she handed the fork to Maverick.

"That was good. However, it's office time. Chloe was there an hour ago, and I have things to get in order."

"I thought that's why you hired an assistant." Maggie teased Beth. She also picked up Maverick's fork and cut a slice off his pancakes. She closed her eyes in pleasure when she bit into it. "You're right, Maverick. You should have never left. The sweetest pleasures are always where your heart is. I guess your heart is still here."

"Waiting on me." He reached for his fork, keeping his eyes on Beth the entire time.

"I'm gone, Maggie. Maverick, thank you for breakfast." Beth pressed a clean napkin to the corner of her mouth, trying to remove some of the long-wearing lipstick.

Before she stood, a couple of other classmates, Jimmy Dane and a friend, also local business associates, walked by their table. They paused for a moment as if surprised.

"Good morning, Maggie and Beth. How you doing, today? You look especially nice, Beth. I do believe you get prettier every day."

"Jimmy, you always were a smooth talker." Maggie pointed Maverick's fork Jimmy's direction. "How pretty do I look?"

"Pretty enough for a date. Marry me, Maggie." He winked. It was a running tease between them, and everyone knew it, even Jimmy's wife.

"And look who we have with us." Maggie turned the fork Maverick's direction.

"Well, bless my soul! Maverick! I'll be. How are you? I see you're in good company, as always. You and Beth always did fit together well. No wonder she sparkles like a new penny today."

When Maggie giggled, Beth kicked her underneath the table. "Sparkles like a new penny?" Beth hissed the words under her breath. When Maggie kicked her back, she glanced up.

"Yes, New Penny. You're a lighthouse of beauty this morning," Maggie whispered, as she boldly winked.

Jimmy rambled on, "I haven't seen you in ages, Maverick. Are you here just for the reunion? That's a week away, yet."

Beth felt trapped. Maverick was at her side, and Jimmy stood next to her, boxing her in. Maverick knew she'd intended to leave, but instead of helping her out, he'd put his arm across the seat behind her and kept asking Jimmy questions. Both of them seemed engrossed in answering in lengthy detail, no matter how inane the subject matter.

When Beth thought she couldn't handle the claustrophobia any longer, Jimmy shook Maverick's hand, blew a kiss to Maggie, and assured Beth he'd see her at the Chamber meeting at the first of next month. He laughed, ensuring them they'd have a good time at the reunion the following weekend. His exit was a godsend. Able to breathe once again, Beth slowly and gently set the napkin she'd crushed on the table in front of her.

"They say old-friends-come-again are the best to have around." Maverick dropped several bills on the table. "Wouldn't you say so, Marilyn?"

"Jimmy's never been farther than the next town. I wouldn't know." She did know she needed some space, and she stood. "Thank you once again for breakfast. I must be getting to the Center. Chloe will fall apart if I don't get there and help hold it all together."

That wasn't exactly accurate, but she *had* been gone several days, and there *was* a core of truth in her words.

Once outside, Maverick tossed her plans aside like a bucking bronc with a rider it didn't like.

"I have a special request of you, Marilyn, if you don't mind. I met Maggie at your place of business, and she gave me a ride over, but I don't think I can squeeze into that little tin can a second time. Do you mind?"

"At my place? At the Assisted Living Center?" Beth seemed flustered for a minute. The Center was her safe haven. Maverick had invaded it the day before, but today she needed its peace and quiet. He'd already been there that morning? Was no place safe from this man?

"If you don't want me to ride with you, I'm sure I can call a cab. Sorry, Maggie. I just can't do tiny again." He nodded her direction.

Maggie just grinned. She didn't seem surprised in the least by his refusal to ride with her.

Beth sighed. "It's not that. It's just, well, it's just that I'm . . . oh, forget it." She reached into her purse for her key, before remembering her new car was keyless.

"I'm with you, then," Maverick confirmed. "Right?"

"Come on. I'm in the champagne pearl Cadillac." Beth motioned the direction of her vehicle.

"I wouldn't expect anything less from you." He blew Maggie a kiss.

"I'm looking forward to next week at the reunion,

Maverick." Maggie waved before dropping into her small car and pulling the door shut. She rolled down the window, her hand waving a second time.

"You bet," Maverick called. "I wouldn't miss this one." He opened the car door for Beth. "Nice ride, Marilyn. This car looks like you."

"How is that, Maverick? It's just a car." The Mr. Cadence was gone. A more familiar name was back. Beth hadn't noticed she'd done that. The casual reference from decades before had simply nuanced itself into her thoughts, and it had come out in her conversation.

She shrugged it off. It seemed, well, right, and no one else had called him by his formal last name all morning. Who was she to keep the calves locked in the corral? His answer caught her off guard.

"Tailored and good looking."

"Tailored and good looking?" She laughed, surprised at herself for doing so. "Not beautiful?"

"You don't miss a lick, girl. That's the Marilyn I remember."

The radio came on, and it began playing *Unchained Melody*. Beth reached to the dash to choose something more modern. Maverick stopped her.

"Oh, don't change the music. Leave it. I like this station. Oldies are my favorite. They don't make me feel quite so ancient. Oh, and thanks for giving me a lift, Marilyn."

"Beth. Please stop with the Marilyn thing. I was Beth all those years ago, and I still am today."

"Okay, Marilyn. Whatever you say." Maverick glanced out the window at the old, familiar buildings sliding by.

"You are incorrigible, Maverick Dillinger Cadence." She felt lighthearted in saying the words, a brightness she'd missed from long ago. Robert had been her rock, but then rocks were never really fun. They were steady and dependable. Maverick was incorrigible and had always been. He was *a* Maverick. She smiled at how little he had changed as she turned into the Center's parking lot.

He murmured, "I see you still remember my name."

"Among other things—" Beth abruptly stopped, realizing where her comment might lead. She didn't need or want to go there. She changed the subject. "Well, here we are. I hope your mother really enjoys living—"

Maverick interrupted her, as if his thoughts had been elsewhere. "What do you remember, my sweet Marilyn? Do you remember the night before I shipped out?" He turned his silver head her direction, and his face was serious. This question had meaning to him.

"That was a long time ago. Lots of things have changed since then—"

Maverick again stopped her. He reached and took one of her hands in his, bringing it to his lips. "Yes, lots of things have changed. I wrote you, Marilyn. Hundreds of letters. You never replied. Not once. When I finally came home, you were married with a kid and another on the way. You never even told me. You broke my heart, Marilyn. You truly did." He dropped her hand.

Marilyn felt numb inside. She had no response. His words took her back to a time of her life she thought cleansed from her slate. Now she knew those awful moments weren't really gone.

The reverie was interrupted when Maverick's door opened.

"Again, thanks for the ride."

And he was gone, striding off toward the Center, leaving a dumbfounded Beth reeling in his wake.

— 3 —

OVER THE COURSE of the next week, Beth did her best to avoid Maverick, as Lily Pearl settled in, Chloe ran small errands to keep the elegant woman functioning smoothly, and plans began to ramp up for the upcoming reunion.

Her efforts were less than successful.

Monday afternoon, Lily Pearl made a special request for Beth to visit her in her suite, as she wished to prepare her a special afternoon tea in the courtyard. It was a first, to be invited for a social call to one of her resident's rooms, and normally she would have refused politely and professionally; but there was a connection there, and with the reunion on her mind, she felt she couldn't refuse.

She rang the bell to Unit 134, holding a small

spray of fresh flowers in a crystal vase in one hand, and a small box of chocolates in the other. Beth might own the building, but as long as Lily Pearl lived here, she would treat the unit as the resident's personal home, because it was. Even the cleaners and meal service personnel worked around Lily Pearl's schedule, not the other way around.

"Ah, Mrs. Taylor." Lily Pearl opened the door a small crack, then she pulled it wide. There was nothing frail about the elderly woman. Instead, she was brightly made up, with pristine hair and an immaculate peach suit over a pale-blue blouse. Her orange patent pumps coordinated with the cording on her jacket, giving her a polished appearance.

"Mrs. Cadence. Are you settled?" Beth smiled and stepped inside when Lily Pearl allowed her room.

"Only partially, dear. Mostly the back room's piled high, but this area is well on its way."

The living-dining area was spacious, but it was the high ceilings that kept the tall, antique furniture from crowding the space. A grandfather clock ticked merrily away beside the door, and a wide sideboard held a large vase of flowers. The suite was one of six for guests with their own furniture. Beth looked for a television but didn't see one.

"We can provide you a television, if you'd like, Mrs. Cadence." Beth set the candy and flowers on a side table, and she noted several large paintings that had yet to be hung.

"Lily, dear. No one calls me Mrs. Cadence, unless

they're my age, and not many people my age are still around. I don't have time for watching television, not and entertain like I wish. Remember, now, call me Lily."

"Certainly, Lily." Beth smiled. This was the Lily Pearl she remembered.

"Come with me, dear. Things are ready outside."

Beth followed dutifully. Tea with finger sandwiches were spread on an elegant but old-fashioned garden set, served under a glass dome, with small screens covering the glasses.

"You shouldn't have gone to this much trouble, Lily." The china looked to be her best, and crystal was set out for the drinks.

"Oh, I didn't." Lily Pearl chuckled. "I have help in every day for lunch, and she prepared all this ahead. If you'll set out the plates, I have the napkins here."

Beth noted there were three of everything, yet she didn't think anything of it, until she heard the doorbell. Lily Pearl didn't respond, and about the time Beth was going to mention it, she heard Maverick's voice from inside the house.

"Mom, are you outside, already?"

"Yes, Son. Come on through." Lily Pearl was pouring tea, and she glanced up at Beth and smiled. "It looks like my son is joining us this afternoon."

Beth felt her stomach turn over, whether in dread or relief, she couldn't say. She turned to see a look of surprise on Maverick's face, just the same as she was certain showed on hers.

"Well, what have we here at this little rodeo parade?" Maverick looked from his mother to Beth and back to his mother, and he grinned. "I might think this was planned, unless someone tells me otherwise."

"I'm just responding to your mother's invitation." Beth held up her hands to ward off his accusation. "I don't know about Lily's plans, but mine are for tea and some conversation."

"I'm glad I showed up, then. You know, this won't be my first rodeo, and I've ridden a few broncs. Unless you keep them fillies corralled, they can get out of hand pretty quick." Maverick set his Stetson on a wrought iron side table, and he joined Beth and his mother, pulling his chair closer to Beth than she'd prefer. He leaned in and grinned. "Are we out of hand, already?"

"Son, you behave. I invited Mrs. Taylor here, and I want you to treat her respectfully."

"Yes, Mother," he said, giving Beth an amused grin.

With Lily Pearl holding the reins of the conversation, the three adults navigated the pitfalls of forty years apart with an ease that spoke to the elderly woman's social position and Beth's years of entertaining her husband's high-rolling associates. Beth was exhausted by the time it was over, and when Maverick escorted her to the door, she felt relief flood her, as she walked the corridor in silence, and shut herself in her office for a few moments of peace.

BETH WAS FORCED into close contact with Maverick two more times that week, once for lunch on Wednesday, when Chloe found some portions of the contract had been left blank, and Maverick had shown up to take care of matters and insisted to Beth that he had a reservation at a restaurant in town, and if he didn't show, he had to pay a penalty. Surely, she could make this a business lunch, couldn't she? She'd agreed, but only if she could take her car. The meeting had run to nearly two hours, with Maverick musing over the menu, then discussing the merits of tea with sugar and without, as well as the best choice of desserts. They'd brought multiple samples, before Maverik had chosen one. Then he'd requested a coffee to cut the sweet from his tongue.

The second time was Thursday evening, when Maverick caught her as the day was ending and walked with Beth to her car. He asked about the reunion, what Beth knew about it, and how long she'd had her reservations to go. Then he talked about his years in high school. He didn't mention their relationship, and Beth felt drawn into the stories of Maverick on Friday nights, trips to games out of town, and the antics the boys on the bus had gotten up to. There were teachers they'd shared, most of whom Beth hadn't thought of in years, and Maverick mimicked their mannerisms and quirky things they'd said, allowing Beth to be drawn in to the best memories of those happy years. Maverick had taken her hand in his and squeezed it, telling her he'd enjoyed spending time with her, before he'd climbed in his truck and driven away.

Beth had remained in her car, with the engine running and the air conditioner slowly cooling down, for several minutes, wishing she'd had that Maverick forty years earlier, rather than the one that had broken her heart. She forced herself to put him aside. The reunion was coming up, Maverick would soon be out of her life, and she could get on with how things used to be.

As she drove home, that didn't seem as satisfying as she'd imagined, but it was all she had, so it was what she clung to all night long.

— 4 —

BETH PUSHED BACK the drapes and peered out
her office window. The clock on her wall showed
nearly five, but the Friday afternoon sun still bur-
nished the sidewalks and flowers with a level of brilliance that hurt her eyes.

Quitting time.

For once, she'd be glad to get away from the Center. Fridays were usually a relaxing opportunity to
wind down the workweek, to sort out the leftover details for the upcoming weekend, so that she could turn
over the Center to her night and weekend staff for
safekeeping. Due to harried staff, breakfast has been
cold and late. Over the day, Beth had developed an
extreme headache. Even her extra-strength aspirin
hadn't taken the edge off, and she didn't dare take a

muscle relaxer and plan to drive. That solution to her pounding head would have to wait. Now, she wanted to get home, and as soon as possible. Perhaps the more potent medicine and a long, relaxing bubble bath would be just what she needed.

Releasing the drapery fabric, she pulled her keys from her desk drawer and unlocked the top drawer of her filing cabinet. Pulling the drawer out, she lifted one arm to remove her purse. Behind her, she heard a low whistle. She looked to find Maverick in the doorway staring at her.

"What are you still doing here?" Beth was startled to find he'd been watching her, and a bit shocked that he'd dare whistle. As her heart settled, she realized how her question sounded, and she smiled.

"I apologize, Maverick. I thought you'd have visited your mother for a few hours or so and then left. I had no idea you were still in the building."

"Then you don't remember my mother. You were at her tea Wednesday. There's nothing she likes better than a captive audience. Today was her lucky day. She had me all to herself for hours."

He smiled and backed up when Beth shooed him out of her office with a wave of her hand. She flipped her keyring through several keys, found the right one, and slipped it in the lock. She twisted it and tried the knob to ensure it was locked.

"Not coming back tonight, I don't guess."

"The staff will forward any important calls to my cell phone," she explained with a tired voice.

"I heard that." Maverick moved closer and studied Beth's face.

"Heard what? That I have important phone calls from time to time?" Beth smiled, glad she could find the humor even through her headache.

"Besides that. It sounds like you need an entire weekend for recovery purposes. Bad day?"

"It's this headache; I've had it since before lunch and can't seem to shake it." Beth was unwilling to admit that the nervous stress of seeing him multiple times during the week may have been the cause of her throbbing pain. She reached a hand and rubbed the back of her neck. "I took an extra-strength aspirin earlier, but it hasn't gone away."

"Here, let me help." Maverick removed her hand and held it in his own, rubbing deeply into the center of her palms. "It takes a minute, but this should ease the pressure."

Beth luxuriated in the unexpected attention for a moment, remembering their enjoyable talk the night before, then she caught herself. "I have to admit, that is better. I don't understand how this is helping, but it certainly feels improved."

She watched him press his thumbs into her palm, as the pain in her head slowly melted away. It reminded her of the way she'd felt decades before, anytime she was with Maverick. She might trip on her words when she had to talk with the man, because she never knew where the conversation would go, but his presence had always been reassuring, especially when she was stressed.

"Maverick," Beth started, "where did you learn this? I imagine you out in the oil fields or rounding up cattle, not giving such amazing hand massages. This is something an alternative specialist might do. I don't remember my doctor ever recommending this instead of a prescription." She thought of the pills she seemed to take every day.

"Feels good, right, Marilyn?" He switched hands, and he began to work on the other one. "It's not a permanent solution to a headache, but it certainly helps. Right, baby girl?"

At those words, Beth smiled. She'd been the youngest one to graduate in her class, and everyone had called her baby girl during her senior year.

"You didn't tell me how you know this," Beth pressed him. Maverick was right about it, though. Her head was better, although not cured. As long as he massaged her hand, the pain seemed to sink into the background.

"My doctor signed me up for an experimental study on reflexology. They used this on me, although not quite like this. I have a rubber ball I rub in my palms, and it does the same thing. I wasn't sure this would work for you, but now I can report back with success."

"This is part of your study?" Beth laughed.

"Nah, that was years ago. I can still report back." He grinned as he released her hand. He repeated, "Baby girl."

The words baby girl also brought back unwanted memories. Her senior year was when Maverick had headed off to the military, abandoning her. He was already out of school and attending college, but she had seen him nearly every weekend, even though their fathers had disliked each other.

It had been a frightful year, with only her time with Maverick to ease the stress. Her dad was the president of the local bank, and Maverick's dad a rancher. Her father had positively told her she wasn't permitted to date the Cadence boy, threatening Beth to the point she was afraid of what her father would do if he knew she even liked Maverick.

A soft bell chimed in the background, the five o'clock shift-change signal, bringing Beth back to reality. It wasn't forty years ago, and she was standing in the lobby of the Center with Maverick. She turned to look in his face.

"I wondered when you'd remember you were leaving the building." He put his arm through hers and asked, "Where are you taking me for dinner, or do you want me to cook?"

"Dinner?" She looked at their interlinked arms and back to his face. "I don't have plans for dinner." She faltered as she spoke.

"Home, then? That suits me just fine. Do you want to drive, or would you rather let me?" He smiled widely.

"I'm sorry, Maverick. I haven't seen you in decades, and tonight's not a good time." Beth disengaged from him, and she tried to put aside the touch of his hands on hers. It was a disquieting sensation, all the memories of how he used to make her feel, coupled with the pain she'd endured. It was as real to her in the moment as it had been decades before.

"Just three times this week. I thought we'd broken the ice, Marilyn. Does this mean I don't get to eat? How's that for treating a man like an old used sock?" He seemed disappointed, and he reached for her hand.

"No, I need the evening to rest up for the reunion. Goodbye, Maverick."

Beth felt her heart pound as she let him out the door and made her way to her car. Once inside, she waited until she saw him drive away before she started her car and headed home.

BETH WAS BARELY parked inside the garage and had the house unlocked when the doorbell rang. She left her things in the car and rushed to answer it.

"Maverick? How did you find my house?" She reached her hand to her neck, remembering Maverick's hands massaging her palms, and she sighed. That had been nice, but the headache was blistering. It was now worse, not better.

"It's not a secret, in Wellington Oaks, two streets over from the new country club. Your head's still hurting?"

"It isn't completely cured. How do—" and then she thought of Maggie. *Naturally* Maggie would tell Maverick where she lived. Magpie Maggie had better not have told him much more. Some things Maggie knew about were only between the two of them, and she'd better not forget it. "Thanks, Maggie," Beth muttered in a sarcastic tone, as she stepped aside and invited Maverick in.

"Yes. Thanks, Maggie," Maverick repeated with a chuckle as he stepped past and walked into the house. He called to her, "It's good to be *home*."

She looked at him, wondering what he meant. Then she asked, "Since you're here, I'll let you help me carry my things in from the garage. My purse is in the seat, and there's a few things in the trunk I picked up that go in the kitchen. I'll need to raise the door so you can fit around." She could squeeze past, but Maverick was too large. She walked through the house, pushed the garage door button, and Maverick stepped into the oversized three-car garage.

"This is a nice garage. I've lived in houses smaller than this. Why do you need this much room?" Maverick headed around the car and opened the passenger door, leaning inside and retrieving her purse.

"Robert liked antique cars, and he had one he kept in here. I gave it to Alexandra, my youngest daughter, and her husband, after Robert died." Beth reminded him, "I have more things in the trunk." She pressed a button on her fob, and the trunk released.

"She's a lucky girl to have such generous parents." Maverick gathered the rest of the things and closed the massive trunk lid.

"I'm the generous one." Beth sighed. "I'm sorry.

That was less than kind of me. I don't mean to disrespect Robert. Perhaps I don't need as many possessions to be satisfied with life."

"No disrespect read into what you said. Some people need things to validate their self-worth. You, baby girl, never had that issue. You were worth everything to me just being you."

Beth took a deep breath as she felt her heart jump. Those were words she'd needed to hear decades before, and now they seemed too good to be true.

She wasn't sure if he meant them or not.

"Stop it, Maverick. Let's head inside." Beth pushed the house door wide to let him past. She was determined to mask her emotions, although she was pleased with his compliment. She led him through the kitchen, showing him where to place the bags, past the formal dining room, and into the family room, where she dropped her purse and keys into a chair. The walls were adorned with multiple family photographs, reminding Beth that Maverick wasn't in any of them, and she turned to him and smiled.

"Do you mind waiting in the living room? I'll need a small snack to take my medication."

"I do mind." Maverick took her shoulders and pointed her down the hallway. "I'll visit the kitchen. You wait on me in the living room. I'll have you something shortly."

"That's very sweet of you, Maverick. Thank you. You'll find the crackers on the counter and cheese in the fridge. Or dig through any of the bags." She retrieved her purse along the way, opening it as she entered the formal room, and she removed a prescription bottle of muscle relaxers.

She opened the lid and shook two into her palm as she settled into her favorite chair. She slipped her expertly manicured feet from her gold leather sandals and rested them on a matching ottoman.

Maverick returned with a plate of crackers and cheese. "Two?" He set the plate on a chairside table as he hovered at her side, holding a glass of water in his hand. "Do you really feel that awful?"

"I always start with two. Sometimes I need more, but today I hope the headache leaves with these. If you'll have a seat, I'll need that glass of water to take these."

"I apologize. Here."

She took it, and he dropped into a side chair. She took a slice of cheese and two crackers, ate them in four bites, and placed the pills in her mouth. She took a sip of water and tilted her head back to swallow.

"You need a break before dinner, baby girl. You've been on those feet all day. I'll tell you what, let me give you a foot rub."

"A foot rub?" Beth was surprised, but it did sound good. Before she had time to ponder whether she should, Maverick stood, pulled up a companion ottoman, lifted one of her feet into his hands, and resting it on his knee, he began to rub the bottom of her foot with the balls of his thumbs.

Beth closed her eyes. She was tired from not getting enough sleep last night, and she hadn't eaten much today. Now, she had just taken two pills to help her unwind. She wanted to have someone take care of her for a change. Robert had never waited on her. He had expected her to be at his beck and call, not that she had really minded . . . most of the time. This was different, and it felt good. Besides, Maverick was a friend she used to trust, and he had never taken advantage of her.

She relaxed with her perfectly manicured feet in his lap and enjoyed the massage. She found herself getting drowsy, and she struggled stay awake.

Maverick had always made her feel secure. She remembered thinking that, as his hands worked the muscles in her feet. She thought she heard him say something like, "This is the way it was supposed to be." Beth just smiled and wiggled her toes at him.

THAT WAS THE last thing she remembered until she woke up to the smell of bacon frying.

She struggled to come awake, wondering how long she'd been asleep. Her platinum and diamond watch revealed that it was only seven-thirty. *About an hour and a half,* she thought. She looked around. She wasn't on the living room sofa; she was in her bed and in her sleeping nightshirt!

Oh, my word, she thought. *How could I have missed out on getting undressed and into bed?*

Why was she in bed so early in the evening? And where was Maverick? Who was cooking?

Beth wanted some answers; she threw the covers aside, pulled on her robe, and hurried toward the kitchen in search of them.

— 5 —

BETH FOUND MAVERICK in the kitchen frying bacon for BLTs. Her stomach tightened, and her knees felt weak to find him making himself at home in her kitchen so casually, as if he lived here, and nearly forty years of history hadn't come between them.

"Morning, princess," he said to her and handed her a mug of coffee.

"I don't drink coffee at night, it makes me . . . What did you just say?" She felt more confused than ever. Then she glanced out the window to see the sun filtering through the trees. When she looked back, she noticed Maverick's crumpled shirt.

"I said, morning, princess, how did you sleep last night?" He flipped over a slice of bacon with a fork, before turning to her with a grin.

"What do you mean it's morning? How can the sun be up? I just took a nap for a little bit, didn't I?" Beth was aghast that Maverick was also barefoot on her travertine tile floor, and his hair was messier than she remembered.

"Baby girl, this is Saturday. You slept all night and just woke up. I'm fixing you a BLT since you didn't eat last night. I thought you needed more than a blueberry bagel this morning." Maverick blew her a kiss and winked as he seated her in the breakfast nook. He went back to finish the sandwiches he'd started.

"Didn't eat last night." Beth repeated the words vacantly, still reeling from the shock of losing a whole evening. She replayed the events of the night in her mind, attempting to pinpoint where it had slipped away from her. A pit grew in her stomach as she imagined the talk that would surround her if anyone discovered she had an unrelated man overnight in her home without a third party for a chaperone.

"I'm glad you had something in your fridge. I wasn't wild about the PB+J I had for supper." Maverick sounded cheerful and very conciliatory, as if he wasn't bothered much by his peanut butter and jelly from the previous evening.

What unnerved Beth was that if Maverick spent the night, he must have been the one who prepared her for bed. She felt herself blush just thinking about it.

Maverick handed her a paper plate with her BLT on it. "What's wrong, Marilyn. Are you feeling okay? Your color's a little off."

"I'm . . . I'm okay," she said weakly, as she raised her arm to move her plate, intending set her coffee down. Her robe shifted, and she quickly pulled the front together and glanced up to see if Maverick had noticed. What she saw made her face warm even more. A myriad of thoughts raced through her mind about what a life with Maverick would have been like: intense, breathless, romantic, complete.

Finally, the phone rang, seeming to wake them both out of their trance-like state. Beth tried to get up, and she caught the edge of her robe on the corner of the table. Grabbing the fabric with a yank, she pulled it tight and reached for the phone, knocking it from its cradle.

"Here, baby girl. Let me get that for you," Maverick called, and he rescued the phone from the floor.

Mortified that the phone would pick up his voice, Beth could hardly speak when she reached for the receiver and put it to her ear.

"Beth, here." She heard a giggle and breathed a sigh of relief that it was only Maggie.

"Was that Maverick I heard in the background?" Maggie probed.

"Yes." Beth cringed at her answer, hoping her friend wouldn't ask her to explain.

"Did he spend the night?" Maggie giggled.

"I'm a Christian. You know I don't do that sort of

thing."

"Did you like the pajamas, or should I say, lack of pajamas I picked out for you?" More giggling filtered over the phone.

"Was it you who did that? I'm so thankful. I thought it was someone else." Beth stepped away from the kitchen with one hand cupped over the phone, trying not to let Maverick know she was talking about him. Relief washed over her, like warm honey flowing from head to toe. She snugged up her robe again, still self-conscious but feeling better.

Maggie continued to giggle while she explained the evening's events. "Maverick called me about nine last night and asked me for a favor; you know I can't tell a handsome man no. Before Keith and I went out, I stopped at your place with a loaf of fresh bread, as requested by Maverick. He asked if I would help you get dressed for bed, because he said he couldn't be responsible for what would happen if he did the honors. Of course, I knew he was just kidding. You know what a straight arrow he is now that he's a Christian and all."

Beth was surprised, but she tried not to let it show. "Well, thanks. That's a relief. And—"

Before she could finish, Maverick interrupted her, "Tell Maggie that when I see her tonight, I owe her one."

Maggie called back, "Tell my man, Maverick, I'll be expecting to be paid in full!"

"I'm letting you go, Maggie. You two can finish

your conversation tonight." Beth hung up, her worries about the overnight Maverick situation moderated, especially with the news of his apparent faith in God.

"Your sandwich?" Maverick nodded its direction. "Don't want it to get soggy."

"Or cold." She smiled and bit into her BLT. "This is delicious. I haven't had one of these in a while, and I'd forgotten how good they are."

"I thought you might like it."

She looked out the window, resting her eyes on the shrubs and grass filling her yard. The sprinklers had run during the night, and the grass sparkled in the early morning sun. Behind her, Maverick finished making his sandwich, accompanied by the soft clicking sounds of a knife on cutting surfaces and utensils on glass and china. She wondered how her life had gotten so crazy so fast. Here she was in her kitchen, half-dressed, eating with a man who'd spent the night in her house, a man whom she hadn't seen in almost forty years.

"I said, how's the grub? Are you ignoring me, Marilyn?" Maverick's question broke into her thoughts, startling her.

"What? Oh, I'm sorry. It's delicious, really. Either I didn't know I was so hungry, or you're really a good cook." Beth's words came out in a rush, and to distract herself, she took another bite.

Maverick placed his plate on the table and smiled at her as he seated himself. "Maybe it's a little of both. I'm pleased you enjoy my cooking. By the way, how's the headache?"

"It's completely gone. I-I-I can't believe that I slept so soundly for so long. If the smell of the bacon hadn't awakened me, I might have slept until noon." Beth held the last bite of her sandwich in her fingers, watching it longingly, then with determination, she placed it in her mouth and began to chew.

"If you'd stayed in that bed much longer, I'd have gone in and woken you up. Who knows where that would have led?" Maverick glanced at her mischievously, causing her face to warm.

"Now, don't you start, Maverick. I mean it. Not today, please. You know we've got a big day and evening ahead, and I have a lot of errands to run. That and I need to get a bath." Beth stopped in mid-sentence. She'd forgotten who she was talking to, she was so used to being with Maggie.

"I'm here to help." Maverick grinned eagerly.

"See, that's just what I mean. You cannot help me take a bath, and you know it—"

Maverick interrupted her. "I meant the errands, Marilyn."

Beth felt herself flush with embarrassment, "Oh, I'm sorry, it's just that after last night—"

"Nothing happened, baby girl. You must know that I respect you way more than you realize. If I didn't, when I got back from my first tour of Cambodia, the first thing I would have done was punch your . . . but, never mind, let's just leave it at *I respect you*. Last night all I did was sit in a chair and watch you sleep for the first couple of hours. When Maggie arrived, I made myself comfortable in one of the guest rooms. Old habits die hard, so I woke up about six and read my daily devotional." He pointed to his phone and tapped the screen to open the text of a book. "Then I decided to prepare you and me a little something to eat. That's all that happened. I'd never do anything that you didn't want to do first, okay? I thought you knew that already."

Maverick stared at her with those heart-wrenching blue eyes, and all Beth could get out was a weak, "Okay, Maverick." She looked away, and she took a sip of her coffee, wishing this weekend was already over, and Maverick was gone and out of her life forever.

MAVERICK WATCHED BETH, caressing her features with his eyes, thinking about the past and having no intentions of ever letting Beth get away from him again. Not when he could feel how attracted he still was to her, and he could see her being drawn to him, just like back then.

When he was younger, he'd have just grabbed her in his arms and smothered her with kisses. Now that he'd let God have control of his life, he had to find a different way. He knew one thing he hadn't told Beth.

This time he was here to stay. Come hail or high water, he was going to get the girl this time.

— 6 —

MAVERICK HEADED BACK to his hotel room to freshen up. He also offered to pick up Beth's dry cleaning and go by the florist before he returned. He said to expect him back around eleven-thirty, and he'd make lunch.

Maverick being away from the house gave Beth plenty of time to bathe and get dressed without worrying about him being around. She first pulled out *Footprints,* thinking this to be a good opportunity to fit in her devotional for the day, and she opened it to the next marked page. She smiled at the heading at the top: John 3:16, a verse she could quote from heart.

"For God so loved the world, that he gave his only begotten Son, that whosoever believeth in him should not perish, but have everlasting life."

She lit three pillar candles, placing two on the ends of the tub, and the third beside the sink. She sank into her whirlpool tub, luxuriating in the gentle massage from the pulsing jets and thinking about the verse. *Gave his only son.* How she would have liked that, to have had a son, for her daughter to have had a brother. Her thoughts turned to Maverick. She had always felt so secure and safe when he was around, she caught herself thinking.

"Enough of that," Beth scolded herself.

She tried to think about other things, the reunion, the assisted living center, Maggie's and her vacation plans, but Maverick kept coming back into her thoughts. She needed to get out of the tub and get ready for the day. That would keep her thoughts busy.

She had just finished toweling off when the doorbell rang. Grabbing her robe, and with her hair in a towel, she ran to the door, wondering who it could be on a Saturday.

Through the glass door, she saw the white uniform of a delivery service. She opened the door, calling out, "May I help you?"

"Flowers for a Mrs. Marilyn Taylor."

She opened the door to sign and accept the box. Inside were two dozen pink roses and white lilies along with a tiara. The note said, *For Marilyn, Class Sweetheart.* It was signed, *The Class President.*

Beth thought for a minute. Maverick! He was the senior class president her sophomore year.

"If you'll hold for a moment, I'll get you a tip."

She held up one finger and glanced back to see if her purse was convenient.

"No, ma'am, that won't be necessary. The gentleman from yesterday already paid extra, plus a generous tip. Thank you, and have a good day." He tipped his hat and backed up several steps.

She thanked the young man and shut the door, admiring the beautiful spray. Maverick had never given her flowers, unless you counted the time she was in eighth grade. He had picked a fistful of bluebonnets and Indian paintbrushes for her when he'd walked her home. That was when her daddy had told her she wasn't to be seen with him.

How did Maverick know she liked pink roses and white lilies? It hit her, and when it did, it was obvious: Maggie. The two must have communicated more than she realized, especially since her friend had known a couple of weeks ago that he was coming down.

Beth pulled a Steuben crystal vase from the large dining room credenza, filled it with water, and set the spray on display in the center of the table before getting dressed. The vase wasn't her prettiest, but it would do. As she brushed her hair, she remembered she still didn't have her regular lipstick, and what was worse, the one her daughter gave her was that new long-wearing, last-all-day lip color. She took a deep breath, knowing her choices were limited to it or nothing, and she applied the lip color. Then she layered on a heavier coat of mascara and even an extra brush over the cheeks with blush to balance out her lips.

She looked in the mirror, discovering she really did look better. The color brightened her whole appearance.

With a lighter heart, she rifled through her closet and pulled out another one of her new summer dresses. This one was lime green with splashes of oversized plum-and-pale-pink-colored tulips. She put on her new green beaded roman-style sandals. She wriggled her toes, satisfied that her pink toenail polish satisfactorily complemented her sandals and dress. She wanted to look especially nice, though she refused to admit why.

A glance at her watch told her she still had about an hour before Maverick would return, just enough time to do some picture rearranging in the family room. She removed several large, individual photos, and replaced them with smaller, more family-oriented snaps in decorative frames. Locking the excess pictures inside a guest room, she immediately felt better.

Stepping through the dining room, she evaluated the vase with the flowers Maverick had sent. She glanced to the china cabinet, debating on the heavy, Waterford crystal vases stored on top. There were two. They were cumbersome, but they would balance the massive blooms better than the delicate Steuben.

Pulling a chair to the cabinet, she stepped onto the seat and reached for the first vase. Before she could finish, the garage door rumbled, and she looked at her watch. Five minutes early, which wasn't a problem, except she'd need to open the door and reset the alarm.

She grasped the first vase and was just climbing down when she heard the house door open and the buttons chiming on the keypad.

"Maverick?" Not even Maggie knew her alarm number. Had he seen her key it in? She tried to be careful, but she guessed Maverick noticed more than she realized.

"Marilyn, where are you?"

"In here, Cadence," she called. It was a high school thing. Everyone had done it, called him by his last name.

"Oh, baby girl, look at you." Maverick drew in a sharp breath.

"Is . . . is something wrong?" Beth checked to make sure her dress was fastened and nothing was out of place, running her hand over the fabric with a smooth and graceful motion.

"You shouldn't be doing that. You could have waited until I returned. What if you'd fallen and hurt yourself, baby girl?" His voice was husky with emotion. He stepped to her and took the vase from her hand.

"There's a second one. I need it, too." She smiled as he took her hand to help her to the floor.

"That one?" He released her and pointed with the vase he held in his hand. When she nodded, he set the first vase on the table and casually reached up and got the second one down. "Will this do?"

"It's perfect, and thank you for the flowers. I'm trading out vases. These heavier ones will suit the flowers so much better. You know they're my favorites." Beth smiled as she lifted the Steuben vase to carry it into the kitchen.

"A lucky guess," he mumbled, as he followed her to the kitchen. There were several sacks of things he'd brought in, including corsages and a boutonniere, that he slipped into the fridge. He emptied the rest of the sacks and began to put the items away.

"You've been quite the shopper." Beth removed the flowers from their vase and laid them aside, and she snipped the ends of the stems with kitchen shears. She sent Maverick to the dining room for the new vases.

After he set them by the sink, he remarked, "I remembered the dry cleaning. Mine, too, so don't go getting my jeans by mistake, okay?" He grinned.

"Trust me, that mistake won't happen. Yours are thirty-six, and I'm still a twenty-seven length." Beth laughed as she let the water run into the vases. "I'd know the difference. You need to start lunch. I assume you picked up those supplies, too."

"I'm surprised you remembered my pant inseam." He smiled, as he laid a cutting board on the table and slipped a large knife out of a rack.

"Oh, my, the things we remember. Have you forgotten the pants the economics class made for all the senior boys?" She felt her face warm at the admission she remembered such a small detail.

"There's nothing wrong with remembering things about old friends." Maverick had out a brick of sharp cheddar cheese, and he was cutting it into wedges. "I don't suppose you remember my favorite color, my ring size, or my hat size? If not, it's seven and three-quarters." He stopped what he was doing and walked over. He put his hand under her chin, looked into her soft green eyes, and said, "We are that, aren't we, Marilyn? We are friends, right?" He paused, waiting for her answer.

Beth's face burned a little more, and she said, "Of course we are, Cadence. Always have been. Always will be. If you'll pardon me, I need to get my dry cleaning to the bedroom." She wasn't sure her shaky voice sounded very convincing as she headed toward the other end of the house, as far as she could get from Maverick.

RELIEF SWELLED INSIDE Maverick as he continued preparing lunch. At least she'd agreed they were friends. That was a good place to start, or start over. He filled the tea glasses with ice and set them on the table.

Back in the kitchen, he opened a package of pita bread and divided one with his knife, opening it to accept his and Beth's choice of fillings. He had a bag of prechopped lettuce, and the thin-sliced smoked turkey was perfect as it was.

He was finished preparing lunch within ten

minutes, and he called, "Baby girl, it's noon. I think it's time you had some lunch."

He waited for another minute. He knew she'd gone to hang up her dry cleaning and, he thought, get her silver glass beaded heels from the closet to set out with her tiara. Perhaps she was in her closet sorting out her clothes and her memories. He chuckled at that. After a few moments more, he headed out in search of his girl.

As he passed through the family room, he noticed it looked different than the night before. He'd carried Beth from the formal living room to her master suite and had passed through the room. When he'd come through later in the night, he'd studied some of the photographs, which were now replaced by others. He shrugged it off and started down the hallway toward her bedroom, when Beth made her appearance into the hall. She let out a frightened gasp.

"Oh, Marilyn, baby girl, I'm sorry. I didn't mean to scare you." Maverick pulled her to him, wrapping her in an embrace. "I called out to tell you lunch was ready. When you didn't answer, I was worried you might have climbed on something in your closet and fallen and hurt yourself. I couldn't forgive myself if something happened to you." Maverick peered into her eyes. "I would never try to scare or hurt you on purpose, I hope you know that."

BETH NODDED BLINDLY. All she knew was Maverick was holding her, and it felt good. It felt right. This was what she wanted, to be secure with her Maverick.

She shyly laid her head on his crisp shirt and breathed in his cologne. He made her feel like he had back then, safe and protected.

It wasn't the same, however. All those years ago, he'd assured her everything would be okay, and that's when everything had gone wrong. She would keep her resolve this time. It wouldn't melt and then disappear like it had done those many years past. She couldn't let that happen again. She knew her weaknesses. She was older and wiser now.

At least she hoped she was.

— 7 —

EMOTIONS WERE CALMER by the time Maverick guided Beth back to the kitchen, where he offered up his fabulous avocado and turkey pocket sandwiches, with coleslaw and whipped cream-covered fresh strawberries for dessert.

Beth took a bite, then smiled and said, "So, how did you become such an excellent sandwich chef? This is the second sandwich creation I'm enjoying of yours."

"Years of living on the road. I wasn't home much, Marilyn. And I got tired of eating out all the time, so I decided I'd learn to cook well enough to make myself comfortable wherever I was stationed."

"How did your wife feel about you being gone all the time? I know I wouldn't have liked it."

The off-hand comment made Maverick smile. He was pleased to know Beth would have wanted him home with her, because that's where he wanted to be more than anything, home with Beth.

"Do you really want to know about my life, Marilyn?" Maverick asked seriously.

"Sure, unless it's too personal. I'm not trying to pry." Beth toyed with the remains of her coleslaw, finally pushing it to the side with her spoon. Their dessert still sat on the counter, with a can of whipped cream to the side.

"My life and everything about me is an open book to you, Marilyn. The problem lies in you perhaps not liking what you read. But here it goes." Maverick started to talk in a slow, determined voice. "Well, our marriage was a little different than most. Things started off pretty good. I met her at the university where I was going on the G.I. Bill. We dated for a couple of semesters and decided it would be cheaper if we married. She was all about a big showy wedding, even though she was already pregnant. I was so excited to be a father. So, we did the whole nine yards. We even honeymooned at Niagara Falls. After our son was born, my wife lost interest in me, more or less. She made it pretty clear that she didn't want anything to do with me physically.

"That's why we adopted Mary Catherine. My wife was already drinking by then, a habit she had before I met her. I thought it would stop after college and marriage. I was wrong. She really didn't raise little Cathy very well. So, my parents had her for a while. Then ten years ago, Cathy went to confront her mother about some issues she had from her childhood, and Donna accidentally ran over and killed her. Donna was drunk, of course. Cathy had just turned twenty-one. It almost killed me. For days I couldn't talk to anyone, and I blamed myself, mostly. That's when I reached out to Maggie.

"Every time I've needed her, she's been there for me. She was such a blessing. She came and helped me through some of the darkest days of my life. Donna didn't go to prison, and that just made our situation worse. Then she started having health problems. It went on for several months before she finally went to the doctor and found out she had cirrhosis of the liver. It was too late to really do anything about it. But I tried. My son Colt and I had her cremated and put her ashes in her parent's crypt. That was seven years ago. So, not everyone can live happily ever after, but it's something to wish for."

BETH WATCHED MAVERICK, who had told his tale with his elbows on the table, in a very casual fashion, as if telling a story that had happened to someone else. Now, he leaned back, raised his eyebrows, and smiled at her. She could see the sadness in his eyes, but she was too stunned to speak. Maverick hadn't had a happy marriage; she couldn't believe that any woman wouldn't be satisfied with him.

Maggie had never told her where she went that

time; she'd been gone two-and-a-half weeks. She said it was a family emergency, and she would tell her about it later. When Maggie finally did return, she had been sick with the flu and in the hospital for almost a week.

Beth never did question Maggie about the emergency. She was just grateful her friend had gotten well, and she'd let it go as of no consequence.

Oh, she wished she'd known. She didn't know what she could have done, but she did wish she'd known.

MAVERICK COULD TELL by Beth's expression this was all new information. He got up and carried his plate and glass to the sink. He set it down and turned to look at her.

"Before you get upset at Maggie, she and I have been friends for lots of years, too. She's helped me keep abreast of what's been happening in our growing little town. In fact, I wouldn't be here today if it wasn't for her. She's the one who insisted I come to this reunion."

Maverick could still see the bewildered expression on Beth's face. She seemed troubled by this new revelation about her best friend. He thought maybe a change of conversation might brighten the mood.

He busied himself at the counter, creating one dessert with whipped cream and one without. He handed her the one with the whipped cream.

Beth looked at the two desserts, compared them,

and then commented, "I remember you were lactose intolerant, weren't you?"

"Good memory. But I still enjoy the strawberries. Now, tell me about your family."

Beth took in a deep breath; she knew it would come up sooner or later. At least it wasn't as sad as Maverick's life.

"Well, there's really not that much to tell. My oldest daughter is an underwater photographer who works off the coast of Greenland, presently. She never stays in one place too long. My other daughter and her husband live about two hours away, and he's a pharmacist, as well as she . . ."

"Names, please. I'd like to know them more than as oldest daughter and youngest daughter," Maverick teased.

Beth managed to get out their names, Candy and Alexandra, and quickly took another bite of dessert.

"Did you actually name her Candy? That doesn't sound like something you'd do. Alexandra, I can see from your husband, but where did you get a name like Candy?"

"It's from her father's side, as well." She paused for a long moment, toying with her strawberries.

"What, baby girl?" Maverick wanted to place his hand on hers to ease her story, yet he knew he had to refrain himself. This wasn't the time or the place.

"My husband had heart trouble. It runs in Robert's family, but I had no idea I'd lose my husband so soon. Maverick, he was a good man." Beth finished and looked away as if thinking about something else. Her eyes were red, and he saw the emotional turmoil she endured.

"He'd have to have been a good man to deserve someone like you."

"Thank you, Maverick. I appreciate the compliment." Beth seemed to relax, and she broke into a big smile.

"Is that what it takes to get a smile out of you, just a compliment? How about your hair looks great, Marilyn, or I like your eyes, Marilyn, or maybe even, you sure look more desirable today, Marilyn. Would you smile for those compliments?"

"Don't be ridiculous. I only smile at true compliments, not false flattery."

"They were sincere, trust me. I don't give my baby girl false words; never have, never will." Maverick moved in closer. "You do believe me, don't you?"

HIS NEARNESS MADE Beth a little uncomfortable. The conversation had turned to a more serious, personal vein, and she wasn't ready for that with Maverick. Not now, not ever, and because of him.

"Well, it's hard for me to believe you when you tell every female you meet they're the most beautiful woman in the world. You flirt too much for my taste, Maverick."

"I've never told Maggie she was the most beautiful girl in the world." He chuckled. "She'd know I was lying. Nor did I tell your pretty little secretary, what was her name, Chloe? I didn't tell her that, either. Who is it that I'm flirting with that you don't like?"

"It's like this Marilyn you keep saying. Everyone knows to whom you're referring when you say it. It's embarrassing." She was aggravated at being put on the spot.

"But, it's true, baby girl, you remind me of her. You have no idea how many thousands of times on my tour of duty I'd look at your picture and pray to God I'd make it back home alive to see you again. I showed your picture to the guys in my unit; they all understood why I didn't need a pin-up girl. I had you with me. When times were really hard, and we were cut off for a few days behind enemy lines, the guys would ask me to show them your picture. Just seeing an honest-to-goodness all-American girl would boost morale. Most of them were jealous, even my commanding officer."

Maverick finished by reaching for her hand and squeezing it gently. "Even now, I sometimes think I'm dreaming when I look at you and see how beautiful you are. And finally, I'm having a real conversation with you, and I'm awake."

Maverick's unexpected revelation made Beth wish the weekend was over more than ever, so she could go back to her safe, normal, and sometimes mundane life. If Maverick was around, nothing would be normal, and it certainly wouldn't be boring.

She smiled to herself thinking that Maverick and

boring definitely weren't two words that went together.

MAVERICK STARED AT HER as he slowly released her hand. He saw her playful expression. He knew there was hope for them yet.

— 8 —

THE AFTERNOON WAS speeding by, bringing the 4Decades Reunion at Wellington Oaks Country Club closer and closer.

Fully aware of the time and wanting to put some space between herself and Maverick, Beth suggested he drive to his hotel, so he could ready himself for the evening and have time to visit his mother before picking up Beth and Maggie for the evening's festivities. The evening's itinerary had arrived in the mail days before, announcing Happy Hour from five-thirty until seven, followed by dinner, and afterward, a Walk Down Memory Lane, featuring a PowerPoint presentation covering the last forty years.

Nominations were planned, and ballot boxes would be available, with different categories just like in high school. The votes would be totaled after the PowerPoint presentation, with the winners announced immediately afterward.

The festivities would resume with Dancing Under the Stars on the country club's outdoor veranda, ending at midnight. Those who could make it were invited to a brunch the following day at eleven to close out the reunion's activities.

It would be a full and busy evening. Beth was grateful she wouldn't have to talk much to Maverick alone. Maggie was meeting some old friends there, and they would all sit together at the same table. Each table seated twelve people, so that should keep Maverick busy and away from her.

Beth wished Maverick a good afternoon and began getting dressed. She rolled her hair in a style reminiscent of high school, like in her senior picture. Everyone was supposed to dress up like they had then. She'd bought a new ballerina-length, beaded-and-sequined dark emerald green dress. Of course, it had been Maggie's idea. It had a sweetheart bodice with capped sleeves, with a scooped zipper in back. All her accessories were silver and diamonds. She dressed carefully, making sure not to miss a button or zipper that Maverick might notice.

She was just finishing her cologne when the doorbell rang.

She heard a giggle from outside and knew Maverick had already picked up Maggie. When she opened the door, she was amazed by her friend's appearance. She was dressed in a dark-pink-and-black dress with black fishnet stockings, so reminiscent of the 70s. She looked flashy and cute all at the same time.

"Where in the world did you get your outfit?" Beth asked, as Maggie and Maverick stepped through the door.

"Maverick picked it out. Isn't it great?" Maggie twirled around to show the matching pink garter under the skirt.

"It's definitely you," laughed Beth, a little perturbed that Maggie would let Maverick pick out her clothes.

MAVERICK, HOWEVER, was oblivious to everything but Beth. He put his hands on her slim shoulders and slowly turned her around. Beth's pale, creamy skin under his tanned hands felt like a satin shirt to him.

"You take my breath away, Marilyn, you truly do," Maverick said softly, as he released her. The rich green of the dress matched her eyes. The tiara made her look as if she had a halo on, a real angel. He'd have to watch her tonight. Every man, single or attached, would be after her, he thought darkly.

"Does the tiara look okay? I really couldn't tell if it's messing up my hair in the back. I think it's silly that all the sweethearts have to wear one," Beth said to Maggie.

"It looks great on you. The reunion committee

thought it would help identify people. The homecoming queens will be wearing mums."

Maverick went to the refrigerator and got out the corsages and boutonniere. Beth's was plain white roses with baby's breath that matched Maverick's boutonniere, while Maggie's was hot pink roses with black satin ribbons around it.

"Ooh, I love it, Cadence. Thank you so much." Maggie reached up and kissed Maverick on the cheek.

"Yes, the flowers are lovely. Thank you, Maverick," Beth's response was stilted, as she glanced to Maggie, still touching and admiring her flowers.

"You're welcome, ladies. My favorite flowers for two of my two favorite girls." Maverick held his chin high as Maggie pinned his boutonniere on him. Beth smiled weakly as she watched the interaction and bantering.

The tension in the room was taut as a drum.

"WELL, HOW ABOUT IT? Will you, for old time's sake?"

Beth knew she was being questioned but wasn't sure what about.

"I'm sorry, Maverick. I didn't hear the question. What did you want for old time's sake?"

"Well, if you really want to know," and he winked at Maggie, and like always, she giggled. Beth thought about what she'd just asked and felt her face warm. "What I meant was—" She stumbled over her words and was glad to hear Maverick fill in the silence.

"I asked if you'd wear my senior ring, like you did in high school, remember? I'd give it to you in first period homeroom, and you'd return it with Maggie last period. That way your parents wouldn't know we were going steady at school."

"Yes, I remember wearing your ring. I almost got in deep trouble over it, too. One day, Maggie was absent, I forgot about it and wore it home. Thank goodness our dog jumped up, and I played with him until Daddy went into the house. I might have been killed, if my parents had known." Beth gave a reminiscent smile. "Do you want me to wear it on my finger, or can I put it on a chain around my neck?"

"I don't care, baby girl, as long as you wear my ring." Maverick's had his eyes only on her. "I'm hoping my ring will send a message to everyone else to keep off."

"Oh, that *is* like high school. You're really going for realism." Beth smiled, went into her bedroom, and got out one of the large rope chains she'd given Robert. She returned and put Maverick's ring on it.

Maverick fastened it as he kissed her on the back of the neck, causing her heart to catch in her throat and sending chills down her body.

Maverick and Maggie winked at one another.

"Well, I believe we're ready to go," Maverick announced dramatically, as he ushered the ladies out the door to a waiting limousine.

"Oh, I thought you were going to drive." Beth stopped on the porch, impressed and somewhat taken aback. This was too much.

"Not tonight, my princess. I want to enjoy the company I'm with." Maverick's took her hand and helped her into the luxurious car. Next, he helped Maggie inside, and finally, he folded himself into the interior, finding his place between the ladies.

LESS THAN FIVE minutes later, they were pulling into the country club's parking lot. It was only a quarter to six, but already people were arriving. Maverick escorted both ladies to the sign-in desk, where everyone put on a nametag with the year they graduated. He then graciously escorted them to their table, where two of their classmates were already seated.

A gorgeous redhead named Susan Hollingsworth, better known as Suzy Q/Suzy Homemaker, was seated next to William Kindle, a.k.a. Billy the Kid. Susan was divorced, and Billy's wife, Wanda, was recovering from knee surgery. However, she'd insisted he go on without her. They'd been married for over thirty-five years. She knew it would do him good to see their old friends. She'd try to make it to the brunch tomorrow. As soon as Suzy saw Maverick, she licked her lips and called out, "Hello, stranger. Long time, no see."

She stood up, walked over, and promptly gave Maverick a kiss on the mouth. Maverick looked at her in stunned surprise, while Maggie giggled, and Beth fumed.

"That's for not doing that to me in high school," Suzy said, pouting.

"Let's go get a beverage, Maggie," Beth demanded, and headed toward a large punch bowl.

"I didn't even know you liked me then," Maverick retorted, while trying to wipe her lipstick off with his napkin.

"Of course, you didn't. Just about every girl in school had a crush on you. But you wouldn't even give us the time of day, because of Marilyn." She pointed in Beth's general direction.

"We were an item—"

"Little Miss Goodie-Two-Shoes was the only one you were interested in, and from the looks of things, I'd say you still feel that way," Suzy finished with a bitter laugh. "But you can't blame a girl for trying." She turned to go to another table, putting her hands on her hips, but not yet moving away.

She looked back at him with a gleam of hope in her eyes.

MAVERICK WAS TAKEN aback by Suzy's attitude. He didn't realize he'd been so transparent either in high school or now.

"I apologize for not kissing you in high school, Suzy Q. I'll try to do better in the future." He winked.

"Oh, you. You're hopeless." Suzy did smile, and she walked away, working her hips as she moved across the floor.

Maverick chuckled and searched for Beth, who had been cornered by Walter Grooms near the punch bowl. But Maverick was intercepted by several more classmates, and it was a good ten minutes before he finally reached Beth.

Walter had been in the band and was one of Beth's neighbors growing up. Maverick remembered the man had always liked Beth, but she'd thought him so obnoxious, she could hardly stand to talk to him in school or at home. Now he owned a chain of laundromats and car washes, and he touted a Vietnamese wife.

Maverick approached and greeted Walter, and then he turned and spoke to his wife in Vietnamese. She smiled and replied, also in Vietnamese.

They both laughed afterwards.

"I never could get the hang of that language, Cadence, not like you, anyway. How are you doing?" Walter extended his hand, and Maverick shook it.

"Pretty good these days. How about yourself? How many kids you got now?" Maverick made sure he asked specific questions so that Walter wouldn't get sidetracked.

"Phoun and I have four, three boys and a girl, along with nine grandchildren and counting."

"Well, that sounds like you're doing okay. It's good to see you."

Maverick put his hand on Beth's shoulder and escorted her toward their table. Beth paused, stopping a few feet away, surprising Maverick.

"Well, I hope you enjoyed your little escapade with Suzy Q. Everyone saw you kiss her." She spoke through clenched teeth.

"Whoa, Marilyn. She kissed me. I had nothing to do with that."

"You certainly didn't resist or pull away," Beth insisted, as she took another drink of her punch.

"I was taken by surprise; you know that, baby girl. I had no idea she was going to kiss me." Maverick wondered what could have caused this sudden jealousy. He'd never seen Beth act this way before.

"How would you have liked it if Michael had walked over and kissed me?" Beth drained her punch cup.

Maverick just stared at her. "Why, I'd make sure he got a check every month . . . a disability check, get it? No other man *here* is gonna kiss your lips, especially not Michael."

Now Maverick was fuming. Why did she have to bring up Michael Dankirk? The man had been his archrival in high school. His family had owned several funeral homes and were from among the well-to-do people of the community. Beth's father and Michael's father had been friends and had golfed together. They got the notion their two children should date. As soon as Beth had heard the news, she'd told Maverick. He'd gone crazy. He had worked out every day, and during football practice one afternoon, he hit Michael with everything he had, fracturing his right arm.

Michael had been out for the rest of the season.

But better yet, he couldn't drive with only his left arm, keeping Beth and Michael apart for the rest of the year.

Michael wasn't on Maverick's best friend list.

Beth had pulled away from Maverick and was headed back to the punch bowl, when he saw Maggie approaching him.

"You better stop Beth; she doesn't know the punch is spiked. I just found out, myself. She's had three, maybe four glasses already, and you know she doesn't drink. Who knows what she'll do this time. One bottle of wine all those years ago, and you know what happened. You're the one who brought the wine."

— 9 —

AT LEAST THAT explained it, Maverick thought, as he headed toward the punch bowl. Maybe the alcohol had relaxed her enough to let her true feelings for him show through. Maybe she was a little jealous of him. He smiled as he advanced toward Beth and the bottomless punch bowl.

"Baby girl, I hate to interrupt the party you're having, but I think you should come back to the table with me." Maverick had leaned down, and he whispered his words in her ear.

"Why? So I can watch other women kiss you?" Beth hissed her words. "No, thank you. I've seen enough of you and other women to last me a lifetime." She took another long drink of the punch.

"Baby girl, Suzy isn't even sitting at our table.

She just did that to upset you. She knows how sensitive you are. You know I'd never try to upset you on purpose."

Beth took another long drink of the punch and retorted, "No." She turned and glared at him. "I don't think you really want to be here with me. You're too preoccupied with everyone else."

"Baby girl, you're the only reason I'm here tonight. Understand, there's no other person I want to talk to or be with but you."

"Really?" Beth took another drink of the punch. Her tone said she didn't believe him.

Maverick tried another approach. "Maggie said she needed to talk to you in private, so if you'll come with me, I'll take you to her."

"My best friend is your best friend, too. You even pick out her clothes. Then Maggie helps pick out mine. If she wants to talk to me, tell her I'm right here." Beth drained the punch cup and reached for the ladle for a refill, pouring the liquid into hers until it was full.

Maverick decided he had to tell her the truth. "Marilyn, the punch is spiked with alcohol."

"What did you say, Cadence?" A look of panic crossed her face. Maverick gently repeated what he said. He paused to let the information soak in.

"You mean I've had five glasses, no, six glasses of alcohol?" Beth's eyes brimmed with tears.

Maverick nodded the affirmative.

"The last time I drank any kind of alcohol was

with you back in high school, and you know what . . ." Her voice trailed off as her eyes reddened, and they began to shine with the beginnings of tears.

Maverick put his arms around her and reassured her the same thing wouldn't happen again. He laid her head against him as he guided her back to her chair. He glanced around, dismissing the stares and whispers of others directed toward them. When they reached their table, he immediately ordered coffee and asked for crackers. The waiter returned with an ample supply of both.

"Baby girl, eat some crackers, and you'll feel better. Trust Maverick on this." He pushed the crackers and coffee toward Beth, and she lifted one and bit off the corner.

She looked at him, rubbing moisture from under one eye, and whispered, "Thank you."

"No problem. That's what friends are for."

THEIR TABLE HAD almost filled up, and dinner was about to be served. Beth was starting to feel like her old self again. Thankfully, Maverick had stopped her.

She knew he would take care of her, now.

Once the dinner started, Beth ate a little and soon felt like nothing had happened. The meal was delicious, but it was almost impossible to eat two bites in a row, due to people constantly stopping at their table to speak to them.

She was aware most of their visitors wanted to

speak with Maverick. They greeted her and Maggie, but they had stories to tell Maverick and wanted to catch up on his life. She'd forgotten how popular he was, and how shy she'd been. Many of her classmates had thought she was a snob or stuck-up. She was neither, just painfully shy. She'd matured early, making her self-conscious about her appearance, adding to her already shy personality.

Only Maverick had taken the time to get to know her in eighth grade. He was already in high school, but he'd wait to walk with her and talk to her. When her Daddy found out, she'd been forbidden to be seen with him anymore, but she would still walk with Maverick for the first block and meet up with Maggie to finish her walk home.

Although she'd never dated Maverick, she'd never been without him, either. This evening with all the familiar faces seemed to be a retreat to that earlier feeling of security, and she hated to see it come to an end.

The meal wound down, and the plates and glasses were collected. People sat waiting expectantly in their seats. Finally, they dimmed the lights, and the Walk Down Memory Lane started. It was fun to see old classmates the way they'd been then compared to the way they were now.

Maverick had put his arm on the back of Beth's chair and was gently rubbing her neck, and she began to relax. She'd been uptight because of the alcohol, making it difficult to really enjoy the evening. Now, in the darkness, with Maverick gently massaging her neck, she was beginning to feel comfortable.

The PowerPoint presentation revealed the classmates in alphabetical order. It came to the C's and showed Maverick playing football, basketball, and lifting weights. Then it showed him being crowned homecoming king. Then the next picture was of Maverick on a tour of duty smoking a cigarette and holding up a picture. He leaned over and whispered, "That's you, baby girl." Beth felt herself blush.

The next picture was of Maverick with his wife and son, and he was holding his baby daughter in his arms. Beth felt Maverick tense up, and she put her hand on his knee, gently rubbing it, as she whispered, "It's okay, Cadence. It's a beautiful memory." She patted his knee as she removed her hand, and she returned her attention to the presentation.

MAVERICK LET OUT his breath slowly. Beth had never done that before, touched him like that. There was a large photo of his son in uniform, and under it was written, "Like father, like son." Beth reached over and touched his leg again as she commented, "I'm sure you're very proud of him." In the darkness she wasn't as shy, and she left her hand resting lightly on his leg. Maverick smiled.

The crowd of revelers continued to laugh and giggle, as well as fall silent in memory of classmates who had died untimely deaths. Then came Beth's pictures.

Beth moved her hands to her lap, making Maverick aware of how anxious she was. She twisted her hands as a picture of her as the class sweetheart, the glee club captain with the caption "Baby Girl" beside it, and then her senior picture with Marilyn scribbled under it were shown.

Then there came the pictures of her family. One was her holding Candy's hand and almost eight months pregnant with Alexandra. There was another picture of her, Robert, Candy, and Alexandra at Disneyworld. Then there was a picture of Candy graduating from college. There was one more of her in Russia taking photos at the Black Sea. There were two more of Alexandra; everyone could tell she favored Beth with her mother's blonde hair and good looks.

When they went on to the next classmate, Maverick leaned over and whispered, "Your oldest daughter doesn't favor you much."

"No, she takes after her father, and as you could see, he was very handsome." She kept her eyes down and didn't look at him.

"I noticed that."

Then the presentation moved on, bringing a round of laughter from the tables around them, distracting Maverick and Beth from their conversation.

Finally, the PowerPoint presentation was finished. Then the lights went on, and it was time to vote on the King and Queen of the reunion, the most changed, and the least changed. Everyone had a ballot, and there were several pencils at each table.

While the votes were being tallied, the dancing began. Maverick excused himself, went to Maggie, and said, "A promise is a promise."

"Why, thank you, Maverick. Beth, isn't he such a gentleman?" Maggie smiled brightly, clearly charmed, took Maverick's hand, and let him help her stand. He escorted her onto the dance floor to a slow melody made for romance.

BETH WATCHED AS Maverick and Maggie moved and swayed together. They made a nice couple, she thought unhappily. Beth was always nervous when she danced. Her husband would tell her to slow down or speed up, so she constantly had to watch her pace, and she'd never enjoyed it. In high school, it had been different. Of course, the only guy she danced with then was Maverick. He had made her feel wonderful. Naturally, everything about Maverick had made her feel good back then, before he had left for combat duty on the other side of the world.

The slow song was over, and another fast-paced one from their high school era began. Maverick escorted Maggie back to the table, and she sat down, laughing and flushed with excitement.

"Thank you, Maverick. I've not had so much fun in months. Woo-woo! You should try it, Beth."

Beth glared at her.

"How about some refreshment, ladies?" Maverick asked, as he left for the bar area, without waiting on a reply.

Maggie giggled after he left. "He's such a good dancer, Beth. You really should dance with him."

"He hasn't asked me, and besides, why would he dance with me when you're so much better at it?" Beth felt her irritation, and she hated herself for it.

"Because he doesn't love me, silly." Maggie froze and looked horrified, as though she'd take the words back if she could.

"Oh, and what does that mean?" The words were just sinking in, and Beth tried to place who Maverick might love. Not her, certainly. That might have been true decades before, but not now.

"Oh, Beth, promise me you won't tell him I said that, okay? Please, Beth, promise me, right now before he comes back."

"And if I don't?" Beth teased, not yet understanding Maggie's repentant act. Then it began to hit her, Maggie did mean her, that Maverick would rather ask Beth to dance. She felt a chill run down her back, and her face grew cold as she searched for Maverick on the floor.

Maggie started to tear up. "You wouldn't tell him, would you really?"

"Don't worry, Mags, your secret is safe with me." Beth was glad to see Maggie repentant. It took some of the edge off seeing her dance with Maverick, although it didn't mean all that much. It couldn't. Their love had died long before, and there was no way to bring it back to life again. She felt bad for her friend's distress, however, and she motioned like a lock at her lips and threw away the key. She'd seen the gravity on her friend's face and would never want Maggie to cry or suffer on her account.

"Thanks, Beth. I owe you one."

"One what?" Maverick asked, as he sat down with a ginger ale for Beth and a fruity concoction for Maggie.

"Thanks, Cadence," Beth smiled shyly at him like she was seeing him for the first time. She was thinking of what it would be like to love Maverick and him love her back.

Maverick glanced over at Maggie, but she was intently staring at her drink. He wore a puzzled expression on his face, but he didn't ask what was going on.

— 10 —

THE DANCING CONTINUED with another slow song, and again Maverick escorted Maggie out onto the dance floor.

Once more Beth sat and watched as the dancing started, until she felt a light tap on her shoulder and a deep voice said, "Care to join the fun? How about a dance, baby girl?"

Beth looked up into the face of Michael Dunkirk. He wasn't as tall as Maverick and was a little thicker through the middle, but he still had that winning smile, and his hair was completely silver, making his ruddy complexion a little softer in tone. But overall, he still had his good looks.

"Why, hello, Michael. I haven't seen you this evening. How are you?" Beth extended her hand to shake.

Instead, Michael made a sweeping gesture, as he brought her hand to his lips and kissed it. Beth remembered this had been one of the moves he'd made in high school to get the girls' attention

"Now, are you planning to tell everyone you've kissed me?" That's how it had worked in high school. Michael might have only kissed their hand, but he had kissed them. She laughed and glanced to the dance floor to see if Maverick had been watching.

Michael laughed, too, as he said, "Well, I guess my reputation precedes me."

"Only by about forty years." Beth pulled her hand free. "But I don't think I'll dance on this song. I believe I'll sit this one out."

"I shall make the sacrifice myself and sit with you then," came his teasing answer, and he turned a chair around and straddled it like he used to do in their school days. "What have you been up to lately?"

"Not much, really. I stay occupied with my job; it was such a godsend to have something to do after Robert died." Beth's voice died away. She remembered how lonely she'd been after her husband's death.

"You must have done something right to get Maverick to come to a class reunion. This is the first one he's been to since we graduated. We've sent him an invitation every ten years." Michael continued to smile, as he talked about being on the out-of-town planning committee for the reunion. "Maggie and I communicated almost daily over the last month to be sure all the details were in place. It seems like everything came together pretty well, don't you think?"

"It's a fabulous reunion, but I didn't get Maverick to come. It was Maggie. She's the one who keeps up with him, not me," Beth explained.

"Ah," Michael said, with a puzzled look. "I must have misunderstood Maggie. This sheds a new light on things."

"How's that?" Beth thought the situation pretty obvious. This was Maggie and Maverick's second dance.

Beth knew from Maggie that Michael was widowed as well as divorced. He had married shortly after high school, because his girlfriend was pregnant. They had stayed together almost eight years, long enough to have two more children, and then she divorced him and moved to the East Coast. Michael very seldom saw his children after that. After his parents retired, he sold their funeral home business and married a very pretty, much younger woman he'd met on a cruise. She died about three years ago from cancer. He still had a roving eye, according to Maggie, and she wouldn't trust him as far as she could throw a rusted horseshoe.

"So, you're fair game, then?" Michael questioned.

"No game is fair if you're involved," came a voice behind Beth, causing her to jump. Maverick rested his hand on her shoulder, "I'm sorry, Marilyn. I didn't mean to frighten you," he said in a much more subdued tone.

"Cadence, how long have you been standing there?" Beth tried to recall what she'd said, if anything, regarding him.

"Long enough to know I can't leave you alone without some wolf trying to grab you up."

At that everyone relaxed and laughed, remembering that Michael had played the wolf in their high school's rendition of Little Red Riding Hood. Of course, Beth had been Little Red Riding Hood, and Maverick had played the Woodsman who had rescued Beth from Michael.

Michael looked between them, first at Maverick, then at Beth, and he smiled politely, as if giving ground to a more able competitor.

"So, how've you been these last forty years or so?" Michael asked politely.

"Busy, and yourself?" Maverick kept his hand on Beth, as if to let Michael and anyone else who was interested know he had staked his claim.

"Can't complain. Did your mother sell the ranch? I saw some oil wells being put in a couple of years back." Michael's question was directed toward Maverick, but his eyes were on Beth's reaction to Maverick.

"She sold some of the land, but we kept all the mineral rights; so every oil well you see on the old Crazy C is ours," Maverick announced.

"That makes you a very rich man, according to my calculations." Michael grinned. "I could be envious of that sort of money."

"I get by," Maverick remarked dryly.

"Get by! Why, Maverick Cadence, it's a sin to lie like that. You're stinking, filthy rich," piped in Maggie.

"Well, the stinking and filthy part might describe me sometimes." He winked at Maggie as he gently rubbed Beth's shoulders, directing his eyes back to Michael. The deejay began playing *Unchained Melody,* and Maverick stepped around and took Beth's hand.

"They're playing our song. Sorry, Maggie. I'm promised to Marilyn on this one."

Before Beth could say no, he was dragging her toward the dance floor and away from Michael.

"Cadence, I don't dance well. I—" Beth started.

"Shush, Marilyn, let me be the judge of that," he whispered, as he pulled her to him and began slow, measured steps around the dance floor. Beth didn't even feel her feet, she was so close to him. She seemed to be able to anticipate his every move as they swayed across the floor.

"Is what Maggie said true? Have your oil wells done that well?" She grimaced. She'd hoped to stay on a subject that didn't involve them, but discussing Maverick's money probably seemed nosey.

Maverick didn't seem put out by it in the least.

"Marilyn, I'm probably the wealthiest person in this room tonight. But you know what they say. Money doesn't buy you happiness; it just keeps you comfortable in your misery. But let's not talk about that right now; let's enjoy the dance."

"I'd like that."

Beth laid her head on his shoulder, and Maverick drew in an uneven breath. Neither spoke for a time but simply soaked up the presence of the other. Maverick finally broke the silence.

"You know, baby girl, this is the best I've felt in a long time. I hope you feel the same way. I'm glad they're playing the long version of the song. I'd be fine if it went on forever." Maverick paused and then stared deeply into Beth's eyes. "Does this night feel good to you, too, Marilyn?" Maverick whispered the words in her ear.

"Yes." Her answer was shaky.

Maverick pulled away and peered into her soft, glistening green eyes. "Are you okay, baby girl? Am I doing something wrong?"

Beth blinked back the tears and said, "No, everything's perfect. I just don't understand it. I could never slow dance with Robert, and believe me, I tried. I haven't danced with you in almost forty years, but it's like it was before. I can do it with no problem."

Maverick smiled as he pulled her close to him again. "You're fine at this. You couldn't anticipate his next step, that's all, Marilyn. You're a great dancer. Don't let anyone tell you otherwise. Okay?"

WHEN THE SONG ended, Maverick thanked Beth for the dance and then had to help her to her seat, because she was a little unsteady on her feet. He felt a little off-balance himself, and he remembered the last time he'd felt this way. It was with the same woman he'd just danced with, only it was forty years and a bottle of wine ago.

Tonight, he didn't need any alcohol to feel this way. It was all Marilyn this time, and from the expression on her face, she'd felt something, too.

FROM ACROSS THE room, Michael Dunkirk had noticed them, as well.

— 11 —

BETH SAT, COMPLETELY out of breath.

Her exhaustion wasn't from the dancing, but from the myriad emotions she was experiencing. How could she still respond to Maverick like it was only yesterday that he'd been leaving to go across the world to parts unknown?

What was it about him that filled such a void in her life and made her so secure?

She couldn't get the thoughts out of her mind, as the dancing stopped in order to announce various awards, including the king and queen of the reunion. Jimmy Dane, dressed as James Dean, was the Master of Ceremonies. Jimmy started with the most changed.

"Our most changed award goes to 'Buzz' Buford Sweeny." Jimmy's voice rang over the loudspeaker, with only one annoying pop of feedback. An employee stepped up, adjusted something on the microphone, and that seemed to fix the problem.

Buzz truly did look different. He was bald, wore glasses, and had gained about fifty pounds. He won a trip to Las Vegas for two for three nights and four days at the Palms; everyone clapped and laughed, especially because he was a minister now.

"Our next award goes to the least changed. Would 'Maggie' Margret Della Jackson come on up." Jimmy held one hand over his brow, as if shading from the bright lights, and when he spotted Maggie, he pointed and motioned her forward.

Maggie let out a giggle as she claimed her award of a three-day spa treatment in Sedona, Arizona. It had a ninety-day expiration date. Maggie laughed and said she was ready to go tonight, bringing a laugh from the rest of the attendees.

More prizes were awarded. The person who had traveled the longest distance was Stella Thompson. She and her husband lived in Thailand. They were awarded frequent flyer miles.

Dennis Milton and his wife won a prize for having the most children. They had eight of their own and had adopted two. They were given passes to Sea World.

The king and queen of the reunion were the last ones of the evening. The names rang out in everyone's ears, "Maverick Dillinger Cadence and our own 'Marilyn Monroe' Mary Elizabeth Monroe Taylor.

They're being awarded a one-week hotel and spa package to San Antonio to stay at the historic St. Anthony, along with a horse and buggy ride to La Margarita with dinner for two, and two tickets to a choice of various musical performances."

Classmates stood up and cheered, and several men hooted, calling for the couple to get up to receive their awards.

Maverick put his hand in the small of Beth's back and guided her to the stage to collect the prize. Jimmy handed Beth a plaque with the event and date, and he handed Maverick the San Antonio gift package. Maverick took the microphone from Jimmy and held it to his mouth.

"I want to thank everyone. I'm sure we'll put it to good use." He winked, causing the crowd to break into fits of laughter, before he handed the microphone back to Jimmy.

Beth was appalled, and she was certain she'd turned a deep red in front of her classmates. Afterward, photos were taken of all the winners, both together and separately.

As they headed back to their chairs, Beth turned to Maverick and said, "Don't ever embarrass me like that again, Maverick. This is a small town, and people around here talk." She sat down silently with her head starting to hurt. She reached for her purse to get out some muscle relaxers. Maverick saw her movements and put his hand over hers.

"Marilyn, I'm sorry. You know I was just joking

around, and so did this crowd. Half of them are so intoxicated they won't remember most of this tomorrow."

"That's not the point. I don't like for anyone to think that I would go to a hotel with someone I'm not married to . . ." Her voice trailed off as she thought about the only man she had ever done that with. That was Maverick, and it had only been that one time.

Maverick turned her face to his. "I'm sorry if I made you feel bad or cheap just now, because the sweetest memory of my life is the time I was in a hotel room," he paused and whispered, "with you. It was what made coming home from my tour worth all the time I spent there, only to find you wanted nothing to do with me when I did. You'd started another life that didn't include me. I couldn't stay here knowing you were with someone else."

Beth could see the tortured expression on his face and felt a small twinge of guilt. Maybe she'd overreacted. It was late, and she wasn't used to being up. Being with Maverick had her jittery and nervous.

"We're both adults, and I guess there was no real damage done just now." Beth paused. "I'm still shy, that's all, Cadence. I'm shy and tired. I'm ready to go home when you are."

"Let me tell Maggie. I see she's dancing with Buzz. Look at Buzz's wife. If looks could kill, poor Maggie would be a dead woman." They both laughed as Maverick walked over to tell Maggie she could ride with them now, or he would send the driver back when she called.

She opted to stay.

Maverick said good-bye to several classmates as he headed Beth toward the door and the waiting limousine. Beth just smiled and spoke very little, content to have Maverick take care of the social scene on their way out of the country club. Robert would have insisted she speak and carry on a conversation with any potential investment clients. Robert had taken investment banking very seriously and had made a good living for her in the process. She'd never had to work, but instead had been a "trophy wife," as he'd called her. Beth hadn't liked the term but had kept her thoughts to herself.

Tonight, it was nice not to have to worry about anything. Maverick would handle it all. The driver opened the door, and she got in. Then Maverick slid in beside her. He put his arm around her and said, "Just relax, baby girl. Your Maverick will take care of you. That's what he's here for, to take care of only you."

Beth smiled, thinking of him being "her Maverick," like she'd called him in high school. She did what Maverick suggested. She let him rub her shoulders on the way home, and then she let him open the door and come into the house with her. He said he'd stay until Maggie called for the limo to take her home, and he'd leave then. That was fine with Beth. She was tired and wanted to rest. The night had been a big strain on her.

Maverick offered to make her a midnight snack while she got ready for bed. She was agreeable to that, and she headed off to change.

MAVERICK WENT INTO the kitchen to pour himself a bowl of cereal and possibly prepare an omelet later for Beth. She returned in a long, soft pink robe covering a pink nightgown. Her hair was a little messed up, making her look even more attractive to him. He handed her a tall glass of milk with crackers to crush in it.

"Here you are, Marilyn. You didn't eat much tonight, and I don't want you to get sick." He opened the package of crackers for her.

"Thanks, sweetie," she said, without realizing what she'd let slip, as she let him put the crackers into her glass. Maverick heard the slip and smiled to himself. Someday she'd say it to him and mean it. For now, he was content to be feeding her crackers and milk at midnight like he used to do after the football games.

When she finished, they made their way to the family room. She sat on the small settee, and he squeezed in beside her.

"Do you mind if I take my jacket off? Wearing this tux keeps me from relaxing."

"I'm sorry, Maverick. Certainly." She leaned to the side as he worked it off, and he tossed in on the coffee table.

They reminisced about the evening, and Maverick

began to run his hand up and down her arm, enjoying the feel of her skin underneath the silky fabric.

"That feels good," Beth whispered, with her eyes going soft.

"Of course, anything my baby girl wants, I'll do it." Maverick kept massaging her arm slowly, trying to keep his sanity, as he thought about how much he wanted to be with her forever.

BETH WAS TOTALLY relaxed with the feel of Maverick's hand on her arm, and with resting against him. This was what she had missed about him, his ability to take over and let her just enjoy the moment. Robert had always pushed her to do more than she wanted.

She vaguely heard a cell phone ring. Then she heard Maverick's voice, "I'll be right there. Love you." She wondered for a moment who he was talking to.

MAVERICK SLIPPED OFF the settee and nestled a pillow under Beth's head. He got an afghan off the family room sofa, gently pulled it around her, and said, "Good night, princess," as he kissed her on the forehead.

Beth sleepily whispered back, "Love you, too."

"Baby girl, what did you just say?" Maverick froze at what he'd thought he heard.

Silence was his only reply. Beth was asleep.

— 12 —

MAVERICK WOKE UP at dawn on the sofa in his hotel suite. Maggie had lost her keys the previous night and didn't have a spare. At one-thirty in the morning, he'd given up and insisted on taking her back to his room, where he offered her his bed.

Now he needed a shower and coffee before he woke her up. He gathered up his clothing and shaving kit and headed into the bathroom.

A few minutes later, he stepped out of his hotel room revitalized. Maggie was still piled under the bedding and out like a light. He took the elevator and rode it down to the lobby, along with several other well-heeled guests, and ordered a cup of coffee in the dining room. Each table had a small rack with a folded newspaper inside. Sipping the steaming brew, he opened the paper and glanced at the pictures.

His cell phone rang. He looked to see that it was his son, Colt. He called Maverick every weekend unless he was out in the field or on an operation that wouldn't allow him to use any sort of electronic device.

"Hey, Colt. How are you?" Maverick asked.

"Fine, Dad, and you? How was your class reunion?"

"Great. Got reacquainted with a lot of old friends." Maverick swirled his coffee in his cup, thinking of Beth.

"The one Aunt Maggie set you up with, how's that going?" Colt inquired.

"Really well. I'll just have to wait and see."

"Wait and see, huh? Doesn't sound like you, Dad." Colt chuckled.

"This one's worth waiting for. Trust me."

"Sounds like the real thing. When do I get to meet her?"

"When I see you in Seattle next month."

"Does she plan to go on the Alaskan cruise with us? We've had the trip reserved for six months, and it's getting close. We can hardly change it now."

"She's going to be there, I can assure you, along with Candy, your new sister, and her husband."

"Right," Colt chuckled. "I recall. They married in a civil ceremony and want to have a formal wedding aboard the ship. There was something about me being a best man, I think. I suppose I need to order a tux."

"Already taken care of, Son. I've got to get back to my room and get your Aunt Maggie out of bed. She couldn't get into her place last night, and she took my bed." Maverick took a long drink of his coffee.

"Has Candy told her mother, yet?"

"You don't know my old girlfriend, my boy. She's got to ease her into it slowly. She'll tell her in good time, hopefully before they have their big ceremony on the cruise."

"That works. The sofa sleep okay?" Colt chuckled.

"I guess you know me pretty well. It slept fair. Won't mind getting my bed back when your aunt's gone." Maverick had used an extra pillow under his legs and only tossed and turned for the first thirty minutes.

"I bet. I was on the sofa for a month in college, when my roommate bailed from our apartment, and I had to move in with Bubba. Remember, Dad?"

"Bubba with the goatee?" Maverick recalled his son desperately begging his father to rent him a new apartment, and Maverick had let him work it out on his own.

"I know you haven't forgotten Bubba. He came home with me for Spring Break." —

"And nearly got you in trouble for hot-rodding down the street. No, I haven't forgotten Bubba." Maverick laughed. "I've just finished breakfast, and I need to take care of the bill. I'll see you later. Love you, Son."

"Love you, Dad. Bye."

Maverick hung up and checked his Rolex watch. It was nearly half past eight. He decided to give Maggie a little longer before going back to the room and waking her. He could fill the time reading the paper and enjoying another cup of coffee at the same time.

Half an hour later, Maverick folded the paper and returned it to the rack. He ordered a cup of coffee to go, called for the check, and signed for it on his room's bill. He visited with a charming couple on the elevator, before exiting and unlocking the door to his room. He quietly opened the door to find Maggie still in his king size bed sleeping peacefully and childlike.

Maverick admitted it would be so much easier if he loved Maggie. She loved him, and he knew it. It wasn't that she was "in love" with him, but she loved him.

His heart, however, had belonged to Beth since he was fifteen. She was thirteen, and he saw her walking across the football practice field with some girlfriends on the way to school. He'd been in love with her ever since.

At times he'd been able to slip his memory of Beth on a shelf in his mind and leave her there. He'd had to, or he wouldn't have been able to get on with his life; but the last few months, he'd been thinking about her more than ever. The reunion had been his excuse to reconnect with the only woman he'd ever really loved.

He stepped into the bedroom to stand at the bed and look at Maggie as she slept. He set the cup of coffee on the bedside table. The previous evening, she was slightly intoxicated by the time he picked her up, much to the disappointment of a couple of "gentlemen" who offered her rides home. But it wasn't her first rodeo. Maggie had told Maverick she knew he would take care of her and would expect nothing in return, and that's just what he had done.

"Hey, sleepy head. Are you going to get up today, or do I need to cancel your brunch reservation?" Maverick stepped to the window and opened the curtains to let in the sun.

"Hmm, let me sleep five more minutes, Mom, okay?" Maggie mumbled, as she rolled over in the bed.

"Take a closer look, Mags. I don't believe I'm your mother."

A slightly confused Maggie turned over to see Maverick smiling at her. Her hair was tumbled about her face, and there were smears of makeup on the pillowcase. She moaned and closed her eyes.

"Did we have a little too much fun last night?" he asked, as he helped her sit up in bed.

"You can never have too much fun, you know that. Where's my coffee? I can smell it." She held out a hand, waiting, only opening her eyes when she felt it in in her hand. "Cream and sugar?"

"Exactly the way I ordered it." Maverick smiled.

Maggie began to recount the events of the evening

as she sipped on the coffee, apparently not so inebriated that she hadn't memorized every dance and award throughout the evening.

"Whoa, Mags. Remember, I was there, too. I only missed the last two hours. Now, about your keys—"

"My keys! Right, Maverick! I forgot where I left them. I remember I had them when . . ." She thought for a few seconds before she snapped her fingers.

"It's come to you?" Maverick laughed.

"Now, I remember, Beth's got them! Since I wasn't carrying a purse, I put them in Beth's so I wouldn't lose them. Will you call her and see if she'll bring them to me?" Maggie looked down at herself. "I can't go traipsing all over town in one of your shirts today." Maggie giggled at the thought of it.

"No, that wouldn't do. Anyway, that shirt would be the envy of my wardrobe, and none of my others would want to be seen with me." Maverick winked at Maggie as he punched in Beth's number. It rang three times before she picked it up.

"Good morning, princess. How did you sleep last night?" Maverick looked at Maggie and grinned, glad she was in on his game to win Beth back to his side.

"I SLEPT, UM . . ." Beth could hear giggling in the background. She could recognize Maggie's laugh anywhere. Maverick was already with Maggie. This was a little early for them to be gallivanting around.

"Princess, you there?"

"What? I'm sorry. I couldn't hear you. I was distracted by Maggie's giggling." Beth knew she sounded sour. However, to justify her attitude, she reminded herself she'd only been up about thirty minutes herself, and she'd awakened to find herself on the sofa, of all places. She'd only just carried her coffee into the bathroom to see if she could start her day.

Maverick asked, "Will you check and see if you have Maggie's keys in the purse you carried last night?"

"Just a minute, I think I left it in the . . ." Beth glanced around her bedroom.

"It's on your nightstand, unless you've moved it. That's where I put it last night," Maverick interjected.

"Oh," she said in a small voice, wondering what he'd been doing in her bedroom. She walked over and opened it to see. "Yes. Cadence, they're right here. I haven't had my bath, yet, or I'd bring them to you. Do you think you can pick them up later?"

"I'd like to come and get them right now, if that's okay with you. Maggie's holding one of my shirts hostage until I find her keys."

"Sure. I'll unlock the back door and put them on the dining table for you," Beth replied.

"Thanks, Marilyn. You're a life saver." Maverick hung up the phone, leaving Beth agitated and trying sort things out.

She faintly remembered Maverick telling her good night. She'd been so comfortable next to him that she'd almost fallen asleep before he left. She remembered he had to pick up Maggie from the reunion and then take her home.

Maggie must have forgotten Beth had her keys, and so did Beth, or she'd have told Maggie to get them. Maverick must have taken her to his hotel room, and they'd spent the night together there.

Now Maggie was wearing one of Maverick's shirts as a nightshirt, and Beth frowned. She didn't like Maggie being with her Maverick so much, especially sharing a hotel room. It was all she could think about as she got into the tub.

Beth was finishing up her bath when she heard the doorbell ring. "Who? Oh, no!" She'd forgotten all about unlocking the back door and the keys. As she stepped out of the tub, she heard her cell phone ring. She hastily picked up.

"Marilyn, your house is all locked up. I checked both doors including the garage. I even rang the bell. I'm glad I carried my cell phone."

"Oh, Cadence. I'm sorry. I'll be right there." Beth hung up, wrapped her towel around her, and grabbed her robe as she headed toward the front door. She hurriedly put on her robe, tying the waist tight, and tossing the towel to the side. She was kicking the towel as she opened the door, and she stumbled and nearly fell.

Maverick offered her a hand and helped her up, and neither of them said anything for a second. They just stared at one another as Beth gripped the collar of her robe to keep it tight around her neck. Then Maverick stepped through the door, shutting it behind him, as he picked up her towel and offered it to her.

Beth felt her face already burning and was on the verge of tears by the time Maverick pulled her to him and softly whispered, "It's okay. It's only me."

The flood of tears came anyway. Beth stood there while Maverick held her and tried to comfort her.

"This wouldn't have happened," Beth sniffed, "if Maggie hadn't spent the night with you."

Maverick corrected her. "No, Marilyn, this wouldn't have happened if you'd left the door unlocked."

"Well, I was thinking about what you said, and about Maggie, and . . ." Beth stopped before she went any further. She didn't want Maverick to know that she was aggravated over Maggie being with him overnight.

"What were you thinking concerning Maggie and me?"

"Nothing. It's just that it isn't . . . well, you know . . . the proper thing to do," Beth finished lamely, and she knew it. Her excuse for not leaving the door unlocked and the keys out didn't have anything to do with proper. She knew Maggie had probably been in hotels with other gentlemen before. But she didn't like the idea of Maggie being with her Maverick where people could think the worst, not so much about Maggie, but about Maverick.

It would break her heart.

MAVERICK SMILED TO himself, pleased that Beth

had some feelings for him. Even though she knew Maggie and he were only friends, she was a teeny bit jealous.

"You know there's no need for you to worry about Maggie. Who do you think wrote me while I was deployed? It sure as . . . well, it wasn't you." Beth colored a little at the remark, while Maverick continued. "I got Maggie's address from my folks and wrote her to find how why you hadn't answered any of my letters. She's the one who broke the news of your marriage only six weeks after I had shipped out, but she didn't tell me until I had been there almost a year."

"I'm so sorry. I didn't know." Beth wiped a tear from underneath her eye.

"I cried like a two-year-old, Marilyn. You were my world. But she wrote me faithfully once a week. It was Maggie who kept me from going crazy over there, giving me hope. And when I came back and saw you, it was Maggie who told me how things would work out for me, if I'd give it time. Part of what she said came true. And when my daughter was killed, it was Maggie who helped me figure out how to keep on living by helping me find something to live for. It was Maggie who insisted I come to this reunion and see you one more time. Then I'd know if I could finally let you go, and I think we both know the answer to that."

MAVERICK WRAPPED HIS arms around her, and

that was what Beth needed. She wanted to be reassured that he belonged to her and only her. She responded by laying her head on his chest and shyly resting her hands on his upper arms.

"Baby girl, you've never voluntarily reached for me since I've shown up for the reunion, except in the dark during the Walk Down Memory Lane. Even on the dance floor last night, I had to make you put your arms around me. And it was after we'd been around the room a couple of times that you finally relaxed enough to enjoy the dance."

"I'm sorry, Maverick. I've had a hard time with this." She had, but she couldn't tell him why. It was something she couldn't tell anyone.

Maverick kissed her on the forehead. "I know you have. However, here you're letting your true feelings show, just like you did before I shipped out almost forty years ago. It makes me crazy for you." He took in a deep breath.

They stood silently holding one another until her tears stopped and Beth was calm. In the quiet of the tastefully appointed room, they let the stress of their lives outside the four walls slowly fade away.

"Are you okay now, baby girl?" Maverick rested his cheek against her hair.

"Yes, I think so," she said with a shaky voice, and Maverick released her and looked into her eyes.

"Is something still wrong, Marilyn? It's me, your Maverick. You can tell me anything. You know that, don't you?" He paused. "Is it what I just said? I can take it all back."

"No, it was very sweet, and I appreciate it. I don't know what's happening to me. I feel mixed up, just like in high school. So many things happened back then that I wish I could change."

"We both feel that way." Maverick motioned to the sofa, and Beth took one end, and he sat down, leaving open space between them. She looked at him questioningly, and he smiled, almost in apology. "The space is important right now, baby girl. I feel God telling me pull back on the reins, so I guess I'd better listen to Him."

"I feel Him telling me the same thing. He's smarter than we are, isn't He?" She smiled and pushed her hair behind her ear, bashful now that they were more in control of the situation. "Everything was new in high school, wasn't it, Maverick, and everyone was just discovering what real love and emotions were like. I shouldn't feel this nervous and scared, not at my age."

"It's not a matter of age. It's a matter of the heart. Our emotional hearts don't understand age. That's why love is timeless."

Beth started to say that she felt the same way, but Maverick's cell phone rang. He pulled it out and saw Maggie's name on the screen. He held it out for Beth to hear as well.

"Hey, Mags. What can I do for you?"

"Where are you? I've had my shower and need to get dressed. Mav, are you at my house, yet?"

"No, not exactly." He chuckled.

"Are you still at Beth's?" Maggie let out a giggle.

"Affirmative."

"Oh, I'm sorry. I didn't mean to disturb you guys."

More giggling came across the line, and Beth smiled. She couldn't be jealous. Of course, Maggie was her best friend and only wanted Beth to be happy. It was as much her fault as it was Maggie's about forgetting her keys.

"He'll be right there, Mags," Beth called out, making Maggie giggle even louder. Maverick told Maggie he'd wait on Beth, and they'd come together.

Beth smiled as she headed down the hall to get dressed. It felt good to have Maverick around again, just as it had years before.

— 13 —

BETH, MAVERICK, AND MAGGIE arrived at the brunch right on time. They pulled up in Maverick's vintage Camaro and were one of the last ones to arrive. They were seated at a long, connecting table directly across from Suzy Q and Michael Dunkirk.

As they sat down, Suzy looked across the table and said, "I'd like to apologize for my behavior last night. I'd already had a couple of drinks before you two arrived. And naturally, Beth, you being the most beautiful woman in the room made me jealous." Beth blushed. "Maverick, you always took my breath away. Now I'll need an oxygen tank just to sit across from you. Please forgive my rude behavior, okay?" Suzy smiled at the two of them.

Maverick nodded. "No hard feelings." He noticed

that Michael was sitting closer than usual to Suzy and wondered if the two were up to something. All those years of military training hadn't been wasted. He'd keep his eyes on them.

Maverick ordered black coffee for him and Marilyn. Maggie ordered orange juice. Conversation hummed as people exchanged e-mail addresses and cell phone numbers. When the waitress returned for food orders, Maverick chose the Cattleman's Breakfast, which consisted of bacon, sausage, country ham, eggs, hash browns and pancakes.

Beth softly asked him if he should have that much cholesterol. Maverick smiled and changed his order to what he had the last time, the three-egg-white-and-vegetable omelet, turkey sausage, and pancakes. He ordered Beth the silver dollar pancakes. She didn't say anything. She just smiled, happy that her Maverick was taking care of her.

Maggie ordered a slice of spinach quiche and yogurt. She announced she was back on her diet. She wanted to look good when she went to her spa treatment in Arizona. Everyone laughed, because Maggie had always been on a diet, even in high school, and she was always trying to lose that ten extra pounds.

Down the table, Jimmy Dane asked Maverick if he planned to stay long after the reunion. Maverick commented that he was thinking about relocating here due to his mother's health. He glanced at Beth, saying, "And for a few other reasons."

Maverick grinned.

THAT TOOK BETH by surprise. She was just thinking how life would be back at its normal pace after Maverick was gone. She knew she couldn't handle him being around without something happening. She couldn't afford to have him live here. An extended week was one thing. She'd lived through it, but barely, and she wasn't prepared for him to stay. That just wouldn't do. Even as much as she loved him, it would be too risky.

"Did I say something wrong, Marilyn?" Maverick took her hand in his.

"N-n-no, it's just that I wasn't planning on you staying here. I mean, our town is so boring, you wouldn't enjoy it for very long." Beth managed to get at least something out, before letting out a nervous sigh. What would she do if he did move here? What would she have done if he'd never left? At that thought, her heart skipped a beat. She closed her eyes for a minute and tried to think of Maverick in her life, now that she had it organized without him.

She knew that wasn't true. She'd never organized her life without Maverick. She'd never been without him. That was the one thing that had brought her peace all these years; Maverick had always been a part of her, whether he knew it or not.

Maverick chuckled. "This town had better get used to me being around. I'm here to stay." He turned to Jimmy. "I'm planning on building a new house out at the ranch and letting Lupe and Maria stay on in the old place and continue managing the property. I probably won't start building until the fall, after I take care of a few unattended details."

Suzy's face lit up. "Oh, that's fabulous, Cadence. You'll be close to all of us. I still live in the area, too, only thirty minutes away."

Michael didn't seem as enthusiastic.

"I haven't moved back home yet, but I've been considering it. Since Suzy and I've gotten reacquainted, it might be nice to live in the area, again."

The whole time he was speaking, he was ignoring Suzy and staring at Beth. Beth checked to see if something was amiss. She felt the necklace she'd put on this morning.

"Oh, Maverick, here's your senior ring. I forgot to return to you."

"Keep it. I know where it is if I want it." Maverick winked at her, making her face warm, and then she elbowed him in the ribs. "What?" Maverick asked innocently. "I know you have my ring, if I need it back. It only fits my pinkie now, Marilyn."

"Oh, uh, never mind," Beth said weakly, glad their food was arriving.

"What did you think I meant?" Maverick questioned her mischievously. "We ordered last. It'll take a few minutes before ours arrives,"

Beth felt her face warm again. She never knew how to take Maverick. When she expected the worst, he always behaved his best.

MICHAEL WAS WATCHING, not quite catching all the conversation, but he could tell that Beth was nervous about Maverick returning to town. Maybe he had a chance at her after all.

He knew she was loaded with money. Her parents had left her well off when they died several years ago, and her husband had been an investment banker, as well. Michael would enjoy having his cake and eating it, too. He'd live on her money this time. She was still attractive and had a great figure, so he wouldn't mind being seen with her, anytime, anywhere.

THEIR FOOD ARRIVED and Maverick handed Beth the butter and the syrup.

"Do you want me to butter them for you, baby girl?" he asked.

"No. If you do, I'll gain ten more pounds," she replied, barely applying any butter. She only put a tablespoon of syrup on them as well.

Maverick looked at her pancakes and said, "What? You'll want more butter, of course. I'll help you out." With that, he put a big slab of butter on Beth's pancakes and smeared it across. Then he covered them with syrup. He looked at the pancakes and said, "You're welcome."

It was Beth's turn to giggle. Maverick could be so funny when he wanted to. She took a bite of her pancake, looked over at him, and said, "My taste buds thank you, as well. However, my scales at home may have just declared war."

"I'm willing to take that risk," Maverick said as he took another bite of his own pancake drenched in butter and syrup, and then he smiled with his eyes fixed on Beth.

MICHAEL LOOKED AT Maverick. He knew he had a fight on his hands, but it'd be worth it if he could get Beth and her money. Nothing ventured, nothing gained, he thought. Besides, he knew Suzy wanted Maverick. He could set that up and then convince Beth that Maverick had gone after Suzy. Beth would need someone to console her, and good old Michael would be right there.

ANOTHER QUESTION CAME, directed at Beth this time.

"Didn't I read in the paper where your eldest daughter announced her engagement and upcoming marriage?" The question came from Billy's wife, Wanda, who had been able to come to the brunch after all.

Beth almost choked and dropped her fork. Maverick handed her a glass of water to help her swallow. Beth cleared her throat before answering. "Y-y-yes, you did read that. But her wedding isn't until next month. It's out of town."

"I don't remember her fiancé's name, or where it was going to be." Wanda smiled encouragingly.

This time it was Maggie who spoke up. "Seattle. That's where Candy's fiancé, Drew Keegan, is from.

They plan to marry aboard a cruise ship and honeymoon at the same time. They don't have much time off, so they decided to do it all at once. He has some government job that keeps him busy, and her photography keeps her occupied. So, they seem to be perfectly matched."

Beth was glad Maggie left out the part that Candy was trying to get pregnant as soon as possible so they could start their family life immediately. Beth didn't want that spread around. Candy knew Beth didn't approve, as it didn't fit with God's plan for marriage, but she loved her daughter, despite her strong-willed ways.

"How did they meet?" was the next question.

Maggie continued, "I believe it was a dating service over the Internet. They've been seeing each other for over a year, now."

Wanda nodded, satisfied with the answer, while Beth had quit eating. She didn't even want to look at Maverick. She was afraid of what her eyes would reveal.

MAVERICK HAD SOME interesting thoughts of his own.

— 14 —

AFTER THEIR GOODBYES were finished, Beth, Maverick, and Maggie got back into Maverick's car. As they drove Maggie to her townhouse, she asked Maverick about his future plans.

"Are you planning to live at the hotel the entire time while you decide what your new house will be like?"

"Well, I don't really see a choice. I don't want to rent a house and be tied up with a rental agreement, nor the upkeep. I don't like apartments; they remind me too much of military life. I might end up at an extended stay residence. At least there I can do my own cooking and still have maid service. My concern right now is my vehicles. This car is one I gave Colt. He's crazy about anything from the sixties and early seventies. I also have my Benz that I usually garage as well. There's no covered parking area at the hotel I'm considering."

"Well, I've got two covered parking places where I live. It's not a garage, but you can certainly use one, if you need it," Maggie offered.

Beth felt uncomfortable. She had plenty of space in her garage, but she didn't want Maverick to use it. She couldn't handle him coming over every day to pick up his car. That would be too much with the wedding plans and all she had to do to prepare for her trip to the Northwest over the next two weeks. Besides, who knew what hours Maverick kept, anyway? He might bring the car home late, and she'd think it was an intruder.

Maggie sweetened her offer. "For that matter, you can stay at my house. I've got a spare room. I only have it filled with my clothes and junk I need to get rid of anyway. You don't have to stay by yourself. Not when you have friends like us around, right Beth?"

Beth was really uncomfortable. She didn't want Maverick in her home, but she also didn't want him staying with Maggie.

"I'm certain Maverick will want his privacy, Maggie. He wouldn't want to stay with either of us. He'd rather have his own place, I'm sure. But he's welcome to park the vehicle he doesn't drive in my garage. As long as it stays parked, I see no problem with it being there." Beth was quite pleased with the compromise she'd made regarding Maverick.

Maverick chuckled. "Well, ladies, I appreciate your offers, but I'm still not sure of my plans. So for now, I'll keep the Camaro over at Maggie's and drive the Benz, like I had originally planned. Colt's coming out sometime in July, I believe, and I want to be sure he has his car."

"Oh, I can't wait to see him. It's been almost two years since I saw him in Hawaii," Maggie blurted, then stopped and put her hand over her mouth.

Beth sat in shocked silence while she digested Maggie's revelation. No one said a word while the tension built. Beth gained her voice first.

"So, what's this about?" Beth turned around and looked at Maggie in the back seat. "I thought you told me you were going to see family in California."

"I did. I was there overnight coming and going. I stayed with my Aunt Ruby," Maggie insisted, defending herself.

"So, you were gone for ten days and only saw your aunt for two of them?" Beth was more agitated by the minute.

"Yes," came a teeny voice from the backseat.

"But Hawaii was beautiful, wasn't it, Mags?" Maverick added, making Beth even more upset.

Beth didn't know what to do. Her best friend was vacationing with, with . . . well her best friend wasn't supposed to do that with her Maverick.

Beth looked at Maggie darkly and asked, "What else have you done with Maverick?"

Maverick broke in on the conversation. "Do you really want to know? You know want they say, ignorance is bliss."

He winked at Beth, making her even more angry.

Maggie spoke up, "Don't talk like that, Maverick. You know that will upset her. Beth, we've never done anything, honest. You're my best friend, and I'd never let anyone or anything mess that up."

Beth had her arms crossed and was staring out the window by the time they arrived at Maggie's house. She was no longer interested in Maggie's "truth." She ignored Maverick as he helped Maggie get out of the car and gave her a hug. Beth didn't even speak to her friend as they drove away.

Maverick headed the car toward Beth's house, and he spoke softly to Beth, "Marilyn, it was a no-win situation. If Maggie had told you, you'd have been angry. Now that you've found out anyway, you're still angry with her."

"Don't even talk to me, Maverick Cadence. This is entirely your fault, and you know it. She'd have never gone if you hadn't invited her. She didn't have the money to go to Hawaii, and I know that for a fact."

"Why does it matter so much to you, anyway? Would you have gone if I'd invited you? No way. You wouldn't even write me, so I know you wouldn't have spoken to me. A trip with me? Impossible. Maggie was my only connection to you and the life I was deprived of."

There was a sharpness in his voice that made Beth defensive. "Things were different then. There were complications I couldn't work out, not alone. You were gone. Your military posting was on the other side of the world, and I was stuck here. You know how my father was. He would have killed me if he'd known I ever had anything to do with you."

"Yeah, I never could figure that out." Maverick rubbed his forehead and looked at Beth. "I sometimes thought he just didn't like teenage boys."

"I think he never liked your father because he was a rancher and needed a loan from the bank from time to time. He said as much once by saying ranchers were the same as gamblers. But I couldn't help myself back then. I was a very shy teenager. You were popular, and you didn't make me feel shy or embarrassed. You really tried to know me. You never made a pass at me, like a lot of the other guys at school. I could trust you. You made me feel safe."

"What happened? Why did you feel you couldn't trust me anymore?"

Maverick had stopped his car in Beth's driveway, and he killed the engine. With the windows up, the silence of the moment, contrasted with the earlier rumbling of the vehicle's massive powerplant, made the moment feel intimate.

"You know what happened," Beth slowly replied.

"The night before I shipped out?" Maverick raised one eyebrow.

Beth nodded yes and felt her skin warm at the

memory.

"Marilyn, I admit I brought that one bottle of wine. But that was to help you loosen up. I knew how high strung you were, and sensitive, too. You worried about everything. I didn't try to get you drunk. How did I know you hadn't eaten that day? That wine went to your head, and you were like a siren no man could have resisted. I just wanted to be alone with you, relaxed, for once. I didn't plan for us to ever go that far. But you made me crazy for you. I couldn't help myself. I was so in love with you." Maverick stopped for a moment, and he tenderly brushed a tear from under one of Beth's eyes.

The memories had come flooding back, memories Beth had carefully put away and never discussed with anyone, not even Maggie. No one knew what went on that night but she and Maverick. And now, here they were, forty years later, with the same memories, as real as the night they had happened. Maverick started to continue, but Beth stopped him. It was time to get this over with. Beth wanted to clear her conscience, or at least part of it.

"I've tried to blame you all these years for that night, Cadence, but I know I'm the one to blame." Beth took a deep breath and continued. "I'm the one who begged you to come home before you shipped out from basic training. I'm the one who told you to find us a place where we could be alone." She drew in a haggard breath and paused before going on. "And, I'm the one who wanted to do what we did. It wasn't you."

"Wait, Marilyn. You can't just blame yourself," Maverick began.

"Enough." Beth stopped him from going on. She needed out of the car, and she opened the door, pushing it wide. She stood, put her hand on the door, and wanted to close it.

She also wanted to get back inside. Being in the car with Maverick was what she'd dreamed of, and now, she didn't want to be around him. The past and all its memories were too painful.

"Marilyn?" Maverick called to her from his seat. "May I come in?"

"I think not. Good bye, Cadence." She closed the door and started for the house.

As she stepped past the front of the Camaro, Beth glanced at Maverick to see his window down, and she stopped to get out what had to be said to clear the air. "By the way, I wasn't drunk that night. I poured most of my wine down the sink in the hotel bathroom. I wanted you to want me . . . and now you know the real me."

With that, Beth hurried into the house and refused to answer the doorbell when it rang five seconds later. She also ignored her cell phone when it rang ten seconds after that. She unplugged the house phone, took a couple of muscle relaxers, and laid down for an afternoon nap, leaving Maverick to deal with her news.

She woke up a few hours later feeling somewhat better, glad to get some of the guilt of her youth off her chest. She'd needed to tell Maverick that for a long time. Now that she had, she felt a release of some of the remorse she had experienced. She'd wanted to be with him that night. She'd wanted to be with him for a long time. Her whole senior year she'd thought of nothing but being with him when he was home on the weekends from college. And when he was gone to boot camp, she realized how much she truly loved and missed him. She didn't want him to leave ever, and she'd begged him to come home one last time.

Then he was gone again. She was already enrolled at the university, and that's where she met Robert. He was a nice young man who seemed to enjoy her company. Robert had been faithful in his performance of his husbandly duties, but never had her heart stopped when Robert walked into the room, and he'd never made her feel the way she felt about Maverick right then.

She stopped and let out a deep sigh. What was she thinking? She whispered, "I still love him after all these years, and I still want him."

It was too late. If he knew the truth, he would despise her for sure. She couldn't let that happen.

No, Maverick would have to return to being a memory, no matter how hard that might be. It was a decision she'd made years ago. She had done it before. She could do it again. There was no choice in the matter. She couldn't expose what she had so carefully concealed.

— 15 —

LATE THAT AFTERNOON, Beth's cell phone rang, and she checked the caller I.D. to find Candy on the line. She answered, surprised her daughter would call her on a Sunday evening.

"Hello, honey. How are you?" Beth asked.

"I'm fine, Mom. Are you okay?" Candy's voice was filled with concern.

"Yes, darling. Why do you ask?" Beth had no idea what Candy's call was about.

"Well, I tried calling your cell and got no answer. Next, I called the house phone and no one answered. Then I called Aunt Maggie's, and she said you were angry at her. So I finally tried again on your cell. What's up? You've never been angry at Maggie in your life." Candy sounded worried.

Beth ran her fingers through her hair and thought a minute.

"Mom, are you there?"

"Yes, baby. I'm here." Beth let out a deep sigh.

Candy asked again, "Mom, what's wrong? Is Aunt Maggie still coming to my wedding? You know I want her to help with the reception."

"Yes, dear, I know. We just had a little misunderstanding, that's all. I found out something that got me upset. I didn't feel like talking, so I unplugged the house phone."

"Everything gets you upset, Mom. You need to loosen up," Candy shot back a bit bluntly.

"Cadence Margret Taylor, that's no way to speak to your mother."

"Mom? I don't think I've heard you use my full name in nearly thirty years." Candy laughed. She continued in a calmer, more placating manner. "I wasn't trying to upset you. But it's true. You come unglued over the least little item. You and Alexandra both need to chill. But she's not as bad as you. Mom, there are things I want to tell you right now, but I'm not sure you can handle them without getting distressed. Or getting a headache or overreacting. I can never be totally open with you."

"What is it, Candy? You can tell me, and I promise I can take it. Go ahead and talk to me. Is it about your wedding?"

"No, Mom. Are you sure you want to hear this? You know what they say, ignorance is bliss."

Beth let out a surprised gasp at her daughter's remark, thinking about who else had said it earlier in the day.

"Mom, are you sure you're okay?"

"Y-y-yes, honey, I'm fine. Tell me what's on your mind." Beth was nervous, worried if something was wrong.

"I'm six weeks pregnant! Isn't that great? By the wedding, I'll be a little over nine weeks along." Candy sounded ecstatic.

Beth was silent, thinking how lost and alone she'd felt when she was pregnant with Candy. Her morning's devotional from *Following in the Footprints of Jesus* was in her mind. "We love him, because he first loved us." She'd loved her daughter so much, just because she was hers. She wished she'd been able to share the news with her own mother, the way Candy was sharing with her. She never wanted her daughter to feel the way she had all those years ago. She slowly said, "I'm so happy, because this is what you wanted. I knew you were ready six months ago when you told me you wanted to get married so you could start a family. What does Drew say about it?"

"He's thrilled, Mom, and so are his folks. He couldn't wait to tell them. He phoned them earlier today. I told Aunt Maggie already. I hope that was okay with you."

"Honey, I'm glad you told Maggie. You two always seem to get along so well together. You were like the daughter she never had. She's loved you since the day you were born."

"Of course, Mom. She's your best friend. Or should I say, of course, Grandma, she's your best friend."

Candy laughed a deep laugh, reminding Beth of another person who shared that same laugh.

"I'm so excited for the two of you," Beth said with true sincerity.

"Mom, I'd better let you go. Plug in the house phone, okay? Now, you'll be here with Maggie in two weeks, and you're staying for two weeks after that, right?"

"Yes, honey, I've already made plans and can't wait to see you. Give my love to Drew, and take care of yourself. No silly life-threatening adventures, okay?"

"Right, Mom. I'm calling Alexa and telling her next. Love you."

"Love you more, always have, always will," Beth responded as they hung up.

Beth sat down and cried, thinking how she'd felt all those years ago when she was expecting Candy, and how much she loved her. Candy had filled a void in her life. This was the next step. Candy was going to be a mother, and that would make her, Mary Elizabeth Monroe Taylor, a grandmother. She wondered what Maggie had thought when she heard the news. Her friend had stood by her during the hardest time of her life. She was a good friend despite everything. She hoped Maggie wouldn't tell the whole world, namely Maverick. That was the last person she wanted to know.

MAVERICK picked up his phone.

"Cadence, here."

"Oh, Mav, I've got the best news. I just got a call from Candy. You'll never believe this. Guess." Maggie's excitement carried over the line like she was in person.

"Okay, you tell me."

"She's having a baby. She's six weeks along!"

Maverick broke out into a big smile, certain Maggie could see it over the phone. He talked excitedly as he opened a drawer and pulled out a freshly pressed pair of jeans and a comfortable shirt.

"I'm going over to Beth's, and either she's talking to me, or she's calling the police on me for disturbing the peace. I'm not letting her get away, not after what she told me this afternoon."

"What did Beth tell you that you didn't already know?"

Maverick chuckled. "Well, Mags, let me just say we were both fooled by her. Now that I know this, I won't be fooled again. She's mine for good!"

He said good-bye and hung up the phone. Fifteen minutes later he pulled up to Beth's house only to see a black Lincoln quickly pulling away from the curb. He thought he'd seen that car at the reunion as well as at the brunch. Maverick walked toward the door and rang the bell. No answer. Had Beth left with someone? He called the house phone to make sure. An unsteady hello came over the line. He could hear in her voice that something wasn't right.

"Marilyn, is that you? It's your Maverick. What's wrong?"

The line went dead. He started to dial the phone again when he heard the door unlock. There stood a petrified Beth, with her body visibly shaking. Her face was ashen except for a slightly red mark on one cheek that looked like a bruise might soon appear.

"Oh, Maverick," was all she could say. He pulled her close as he shut the door behind him. She wasn't crying, which was unusual for Beth. She was so sensitive that Maverick knew she would normally be in a torrent of tears. Something was terribly wrong with the whole situation.

"What happened? Baby girl, who did this to you?" Maverick's voice had an edge to it, yet he was strangely calm. Beth just lay against him not saying a word. He could tell she was scared and had probably never been this frightened in her life.

He wished she felt she could tell him the truth.

"I answered the door without checking to see who it was, because I thought it was you." Beth's voice continued to shake. "He came in and tried to kiss me. He'd been drinking, and then he, he . . ." Beth stopped and pressed herself closer to Maverick.

Maverick knew she was avoiding his question.

"Who did this to you, Marilyn?" he insisted in a steely voice. He peered into her soft green orbs, trying to discern any hint of what had taken place. The ugly red mark on her face made his blood pressure skyrocket. Somebody was going to pay for this.

Beth took a deep breath and whispered in his ear, "I can't tell you. He threatened me, and he meant it, Maverick."

Maverick separated from Beth. He stared at her furiously and spoke between clenched teeth. "I mean it, too. You'd better tell me. No one is going to ever hurt my Marilyn without living to regret it. I'm calling the police."

"He told me if I called the police, he'd would hurt me even worse. Neither you nor the police can protect me all the time. He'll do something to destroy you, and you'll hate me for it. He said he'd do it." Beth was starting to cry softly with large tears dripping down her red-stained cheeks.

"How can he make me hate you, Marilyn? No one could ever do that." Maverick put his hand under her chin. "Just give me a name, baby girl. That's all I ask, just a name."

— 16 —

MAVERICK COULD HEAR the hopelessness in
Beth's voice and see the misery in her face. He
couldn't understand how she could be so afraid.
Nothing anyone could say would change his heart.
He'd tried to block out Beth for the last forty years.
He'd married, raised a family, worked a sixty-hour-a-
week job, and stayed as far away from her as he pos-
sibly could.

But Beth would be there, haunting his dreams two
or three times a week, reliving that last night before
shipping out, or in the backseat of his car, making
out. Or, he would hear a song that reminded him of
her. He would smell another woman wearing Beth's
cologne. Finally, when he couldn't take it any longer,
he would call Maggie and listen to her giggle. Only

then could he calm down and keep going, knowing that the person he was talking to would also be talking to Beth. And now that he had finally decided to give love one more try, someone was threatening to destroy them. He couldn't, no, he wouldn't let that happen. He had come too far with Beth over the past few days to let someone stop him now. He would go Rambo on them before he let that happen.

Maverick looked at Beth and calmly said, "I'm moving in. If you don't like it, call the police. That's the only way you'll get me to leave. No one, and I mean no one is ever going to make my Marilyn afraid."

BETH STARED BACK at Maverick and knew it was useless to argue. She gave out a defeated sigh. Besides, she could feel a headache coming on, and she didn't want to take any more muscle relaxers; she'd already had two today. And an argument with Maverick would put a headache into full swing.

Maverick gave her a hug and whispered in her ear, "I can tell you're stressed. You probably haven't eaten since the brunch. Do you think you could eat something, baby girl? I think that might help you." His voice was gentle, and he reached and rubbed the back of her neck, causing her to almost melt.

Maverick's hands felt so good.

Beth shook herself. What was she doing? She should be upset and yelling at the thought of Maverick trying to move in instead of thinking how nice it would be to have Maverick massage her daily and how secure she would feel knowing that he'd be here to take care of her and protect her.

"Yes, maybe I should eat something. Just crackers and milk, okay, Cadence?" Beth replied, as she forced herself away from Maverick's powerful touch. She headed toward the kitchen.

"Whatever you say, Marilyn." Maverick followed her. He got out the things for her snack, pouring himself some cereal with soymilk.

"Park your car in the garage. I don't want the neighbors to know you're here," Beth said, as she started eating.

"Sure, baby girl. I planned on doing that. I don't want anyone to know I'm here, not even Maggie, alright?"

Beth breathed a sigh of relief. She didn't want Maggie to know Maverick was living here, either.

Beth didn't look at Maverick until she finished her crackers and milk. She could feel his eyes on her, and she couldn't face him knowing she didn't intend to give him the information he wanted. When she finally did glance his way, she could see the hurt and disappointment in his eyes. She knew she was responsible for it.

She had only seen this expression one other time, and that was when he returned from his tour of duty. He had begged her to let him see her. She made sure Candy was taking her afternoon nap and Robert was at work. She had been about six months pregnant with

Alexandra. Beth had talked Maggie into leaving work early to be with her, too. Maverick had come by the house and stayed for about fifteen minutes.

He told her then how much she'd hurt him, but he would always care about her. However, he wouldn't treat Robert the way he'd been treated. He knew Beth must love Robert to marry so soon and start a family so quickly. Maverick left that day after saying he was determined not to undermine Beth's marriage or the life she had without him.

Beth never forgot the look in his eyes that day, and here it was again. She was putting Maverick through suffering he didn't deserve.

"Maverick—" Beth started softly.

"DON'T EVEN START, Marilyn. Saying you're sorry doesn't help now, just like it didn't help then."

Maverick spoke in a heated voice. He'd been thinking during the silence as well, and he had to let some things go. Beth would need to understand him better.

"All I've ever wanted since I was fifteen years old was to make you happy and to make you mine. But you don't trust me to do the right thing. How can I fix what I don't know is broken? Marilyn, you're the reason I signed up in the first place. I knew I was a poor cattle rancher's son, and you were the rich banker's daughter. I didn't have enough money to finish my college education without going into debt. I thought if I chose the military that your family would respect me, and I could finish my education on the G.I. Bill and make a decent living for you. Then maybe your father would esteem me worthy enough to marry you. That's why I went to war, so I could marry you.

"But you didn't trust me enough to wait on me. You got scared, married someone else and had a life without me. Now here I am again, wanting to help, and you still won't let me in your life." Maverick broke away angrily and strode from the kitchen. He called back, "You want a life without me, then you've got it. I can't try anymore. Keep your life and your secrets. I hope they keep you warm at night." With a frustrated sigh, he opened the front door and left.

Maverick was angry, but not as angry as he let Beth believe. He'd already decided to take care of the dark Lincoln himself, without involving her. If he stayed at her house, it might be a little too risky. He got into his car and started making phone calls. Let Marilyn play her own hand. He had to know if she loved him the way he loved her.

INSIDE HER LARGE, luxurious home, a devastated Beth sat in her family room feeling completely devoid of life. She felt a cold chill through her entire body. She had finally done it. She had finally gotten Maverick to not love her anymore. It was the loneliest feeling she had ever experienced, leaving her empty, like part of her had died.

She hadn't felt this way, even after Robert passed away. She missed Robert's companionship, certainly, but little else. That's all she'd ever thought of him as, a husband and companion.

Maverick had been her lover, someone she ached for during the nights, longing for the taste of his mouth and hungry for his kisses. She had been restless with the thought of him, craving him at times so badly she had reached out to Robert, only to be disappointed.

Now Maverick was gone, and it was her fault. She began to panic. She was truly scared.

What would life be without her Maverick?

— 17 —

MAGGIE ANSWERED HER phone, shocked to hear Beth's voice on the other end. She thought Beth was angry with her.

"You've got to come over here, now!" That was the most desperate Beth had sounded in years.

"I'm on my way." Maggie couldn't imagine what could have Beth so upset without it involving Maverick. She made a phone call while en route to Beth's. Maverick picked up his cell phone.

"Cadence here," came his usual greeting.

"Is there something I should know before I arrive at Beth's in five minutes?" Maggie asked.

"Why, what makes you think something is wrong?" Maverick drawled, checking his watch. "By the way, I've been gone from Beth's fifteen minutes."

"Maverick, what did you do to make Beth call me and beg me to come immediately? She sounded desperate. What was worse, she wasn't crying, she was that upset. She totally ignored the fact that she's been angry with me."

Maverick briefly told her what was going on and about the dark Lincoln. He made Maggie promise not to say a word. They finished talking just as Maggie pulled into Beth's drive.

Beth was waiting for Maggie at the door when she got there. One look at Beth's tortured expression told Maggie this was serious.

"Promise me you won't say a word to Maverick. I mean it, if you want to stay my friend. You have to promise, not a word, peep or mutter," was the first thing out of Beth's mouth.

"Of course, I won't tell Maverick, if you don't want me to," Maggie said sincerely, while thinking to herself, *Unless it's for your own good.*

Beth dropped into a chair like a lead weight. "I probably shouldn't tell you, but I have to tell someone, and the only other person I've ever confided in is Candy, and I certainly can't tell her."

"And?" Maggie saw the tears coming, and she handed her friend a box of tissues.

Beth just sat silently staring at nothing, just taking in a deep sigh and dabbing at her eyes. Finally, Maggie spoke up.

"Well, what is it, and what happened to your face? Did Maverick do that?" Maggie tried to sound suspicious and accusing.

Beth immediately defended him. "Don't be ridiculous! Of course not. You know my Maverick would never do anything to hurt me."

Maggie smiled to herself, knowing it was true. Maverick would never hurt a woman, especially not Beth. Maggie was reassured by Beth's reaction.

"Then what did happen, and why did you call me to rush straight over, if nothing's wrong?" Maggie took Beth's mangled tissue and offered her another one.

"You promise you won't say a word?" Beth pleaded with Maggie.

"I've already said I wouldn't. What is it?" Now she was starting to worry. This was sounding more serious than she first thought.

Beth took a deep breath and barely made an audible whisper, "It was Michael."

"Michael Dunkirk?"

"Yes. He knows everything, and I mean everything," Beth blurted in a rush of words. "And he's going to tell Maverick if I don't do what he wants. If my Maverick finds out, he'll hate me for eternity. Oh Maggie, I think he already does. I think I've lost Maverick forever."

A torrent of tears that had no intention of stopping started down Beth's face.

"No matter what happened in my life, I was always comforted by what Maverick said that last time we spoke. Remember when he came home and said good-bye to me?" Beth asked through the tears.

Maggie nodded yes.

"He said he'd always care about me. But I made him change his mind today. And it's all my fault."

Maggie wasn't troubled about Maverick. She knew how he felt about Beth, so she tried to focus her.

"How does Michael know?" This was what had Maggie concerned and nervous.

Beth slowly dried her tears for a moment and tried to regain her composure. "Remember his first wife was a nurse's aide at the County Hospital? She was getting her training to be a nurse. Well, apparently she was in the room attending while I was delivering Candy. When the labor got intense, I started yelling for Maverick," Beth stated quietly.

"There's no way. I was the only one in that room besides the doctor. And yes, you did yell for Maverick, but no one heard you but me and the doctor. That's why I never mentioned it. The doctor asked if he was the baby's father, and I said yes. I was thankful he didn't ask if he was your husband. He commented that it was an unusual name and then let the nurse in to clean up." Maggie felt like an idiot as she suddenly remembered. "The nurse was standing in the corner observing. She never did anything until the baby was delivered. I didn't think about her being there. But it couldn't have been her. This was a nurse, not an aide."

Beth just stared at Maggie, as if unsure why she

didn't understand. "It was decades ago, Maggie. Things were different then. Maybe she was doing it for part of her training. All I know is that Michael knows the truth. His comment to me was, 'Well, at least my ex was good for something.' He's going to tell Maverick the truth, and now it probably won't matter because he doesn't love me anymore, anyway."

Beth started to cry again as Maggie sat and thought about what she'd just heard. This made things more complicated, but it was time.

Maggie took her friend's hand. "Well, Beth, have you thought about the truth? Have you ever once thought about just sitting down with Maverick and telling him the honest-to-goodness truth? I believe he can take it, and I don't think he'll hate you. And you said you have nothing to lose anymore."

Beth replied while still trying to stop the tears, and her words came out in a muffled sob. "Of course, he'll hate me. I wasn't honest with him. I couldn't take a chance on losing everything. Even now it would still hurt people I love. I don't think I can ever do that."

Maggie was getting aggravated. Beth needed to be reasonable, and Maggie sniped, "So, it would be easier to let some jerk threaten you with doing whatever he says when he says it rather than to just tell Maverick the truth? When did Maverick ever let you down or turn his back on you? Never. You did it to him forty years ago, and you're doing it to him again because of Michael. Think about what you're doing, Beth, and for once in your life, follow your heart!"

Maggie put her arms around Beth. She loved her, but Beth needed to hear the truth.

Beth whispered, "I can't tell Maverick that I let him believe a lie. You don't do that to people you love."

Maggie heard what she suspected all along. She had just listened to the confession with her own two ears.

Beth had never stopped loving Maverick.

— 18 —

MAVERICK PARKED AND locked his car in a well-lighted area of the hotel parking lot. As he stepped into the lobby, the concierge motioned for him to approach.

"Yes, what can I do for you?" Maverick had his key already out and a bag of dry cleaning over his shoulder.

"Sir," the concierge shared, "a woman was asking to be let into your room. She said it was supposed to be a surprise. I told her we couldn't do that without your permission. She seemed angry and said she'd wait for you at the bar. I hope I didn't do the wrong thing."

"No, never let anyone into my room unless I'm with them or tell you otherwise. Thank you for following my requests." Maverick handed the gentleman a fifty-dollar tip.

The concierge thanked him profusely.

"By the way," Maverick asked, "she wouldn't by any chance be a redhead?" The concierge nodded yes. "Perfect," Maverick said and walked in the direction of the bar.

Suzy Q sat in a dimly lit corner of the bar. She was dressed in a very flimsy, revealing blouse and low-rise shorts revealing a sliver of a very tanned tummy. She'd been drinking but didn't appear to be drunk. As soon as she saw Maverick, she yelled out, "Over here, handsome."

Maverick walked across the room evaluating the situation. He wasn't sure, but he suspected what she wanted. He might have wanted it years ago, but he now had a relationship with God, and there was only one woman he desired. He sat across from her, gently placing his dry cleaning on the seat at his side.

"I've been waiting for you forever," Suzy said to him, "or at least for forty years. I was afraid you'd bring Miss Goodie-Two-Shoes with you, but then she wouldn't be Miss Goodie-Two-Shoes if she'd done that." Suzy laughed at her witty quip.

Maverick shook his head, and he wrapped his fingers into a double fist and rested them on the table. "Suzy, Suzy, I hate to hear you say that. It's mean of you, and you're better than that."

"Come now, Mav, how do you know I'm better than that?" She lifted the tumbler before her and downed a swig.

He quizzed her in a very somber tone, "So, you were trying to get into my room? What could you possibly want in my room?"

She colored and wiped her hand on her shorts, to remove the dampness from the glass. "It was just old times, Mav. I wanted to surprise you. I've been waiting for a long time for a man like you." She reached forward, wrapped her hands around his, pressed her ankle against his leg under the table, and twisted her foot slightly to ensure he could feel it.

Maverick had no trouble understanding her intentions. He pulled his hands away, dismissing the overture. "Well, thank you for the compliment, but I believe I'll pass. There's a better way, Suzy, God's way. He lives here, and I couldn't do what you want." Maverick tapped his chest as he spoke. "And you're right; Marilyn would never have accompanied me here. She has upstanding, Christian morals, something a lot of people have forgotten about. Be sure and tell that to Michael when you see him."

"Why, how can you say that? You think Michael could convince me to come here? Maverick, I'm hurt."

She reached for his arm with her fingertips, only to have him move his elbows out of her way, to rest them on the back of the bench seat.

"He did, didn't he?"

Suzy puckered her mouth into a petulant sulk, and when Maverick didn't yield, she laughed and turned her head to look at the people in the rest of the bar.

"Well, it seemed like a good idea at the time. I'm sorry, Maverick, and embarrassed that Michael talked me into this."

"What did he promise you? Suzy, you're beautiful and better than this. Go home. Wake up in the morning glad you didn't follow through on this nonsense."

"You've said it twice, so it must be true." She looked really embarrassed, like she'd sink into the floor, if she could.

"What's that?" Maverick smiled.

"I'm better than this, and you know, I am. Riding in Michael's Lincoln does things to a girl, and now I feel foolish, with you being all gentleman. I have a bitter bill to swallow, and if you don't mind, I'll walk away while I still have a little pride left."

"You do that, darlin'. Here, for a taxi to get you home." Maverick offered her a fifty and stepped aside as she got up and left the bar.

He'd had just reached his room when his phone rang. He glanced at the display and answered it.

"Hey, Mags. What's up?"

"I know you just got back to the hotel, but you'd better do something quick. Beth thinks you hate her, and it's all her fault. I've never seen her this depressed, ever. She thinks she's lost you forever. She looks so despondent. You need to make nice and fix this up. Let her know things are okay between you two. I'm afraid she'll take too many of those muscle relaxers of hers and that will be the end."

Maverick asked, "Did she say she might do anything like that?"

"No, but you know how she is. She's not thinking clearly right now."

"All I want is for Marilyn to finally decide how she feels about me. If it's the same as it was then, I'm hers. If not, I need to know. I can't go on hoping she'll love me someday." Maverick hung his clothes, tossed his key on the bed, and sat beside it. "And did she say who the jerk was that threatened her and did that to her?"

"I want to tell you, Maverick, but Beth wouldn't forgive me." She paused, saying nothing else into the phone.

"I don't care what you told Marilyn. Tell me who it is," Maverick demanded.

"I promised her I wouldn't tell, and I won't break the promise. But you know who it is."

"That's all I need to know. He's a dead man."

"And one other thing Beth said, something I thought you might, maybe, perhaps be interested in," Maggie said in a more playful voice.

"It can wait. I have something, rather *someone* I need to attend to."

"Even if Beth said she loved you?" Maggie questioned.

"What?" Maverick nearly shouted. This added a whole new dimension to the situation. "She said it, you're sure?" He was excited beyond belief.

"Yes, she said that she loved you, and that she'd

deceived you, and you would never love her or trust her because of this one thing." Maggie giggled, fueling even more of Maverick's enthusiasm.

"All the more reason to take care of business. No one is ever going to threaten or hurt Marilyn as long as I'm alive."

Maggie cautioned him, "But don't do something that'll get you into trouble or that you'll regret. I couldn't handle knowing something happened to you because of what I said. You've got a lot to live for now."

"Don't you think I know it? I won't blow this. I'll just make a certain someone sorry he ever came to the reunion."

Maverick then continued to tell Maggie about Suzy Q as well. Maggie was shocked that Suzy Q would try such a thing.

"Well, I'm glad the concierge didn't let her in. No telling what she would have tried to blame on you."

"Exactly, and with the state Marilyn's in, that's all she would have needed to decide I didn't love her. Maggie, take care of my girl. I'll be gone a couple of days. When I return, everything'll be okay. I promise. Don't worry about me. Just take care of my baby girl, okay, best-friend-a-Maverick-could-ever-have?"

MAGGIE LAUGHED AND agreed. Poor lovesick Maverick sounded silly, pleading on the phone. Of course, she would take care of Beth, she assured him. Beth was her best friend. She didn't need Maverick to remind her to do that. She'd been taking care of Beth since grade school, when she found out she could talk; she'd been just too shy to. Maggie had been Beth's voice for the last fifty years or so. She wouldn't stop taking care of her just because Maverick was back in the picture. That would just make it more exciting.

And if there was one thing Beth needed more in her life, according to Maggie, it was excitement. With Maverick around, Maggie was sure they would have plenty of it.

— 19 —

BETH NUZZLED HER pillow, enjoying Maverick's strong hands as they massaged her bare shoulders. Then he whispered that he loved her and gently kissed her neck.

The alarm went off, and she woke up from another nightmare.

Any dream Maverick was in was now a nightmare to Beth. She couldn't seem to get him out of her thoughts, day or night. It was Tuesday morning, and she hadn't heard from or seen him since Sunday evening, when he had said he was leaving her for good.

She had half hoped for, half dreaded Maverick's appearance at Shadetree Assisted Living Center to visit his mother. But he hadn't shown up, according to Chloe, who had kept an eye out for him.

"Oh, Beth," Chloe said, when Beth had asked her about Maverick the previous day. "I noticed how good you two looked together, and with your sad face this week, I knew he must be the reason. He's such a handsome man. Not many older gentlemen carry themselves so well. You two would be perfect together. I'll notify you right away if he shows."

"Stop that, Chloe. I just have a few forms for him to go over." She dismissed her assistant's assumptions, but her description of Maverick made her ache for him.

Beth was applying her makeup when her house phone rang. She checked the caller I.D. to find a number from an unknown area code, and she let it go to voice mail.

A few seconds later her cell phone rang with the same unknown area code. Irritated, she didn't answer it either, as she was running late to work. She could check the message on the way to the office, and if they didn't leave one, it wasn't important, anyway.

She got in the car with her cup of coffee and put her phone on speaker. The message was from Michael. He said that he had tried her at home but couldn't get her, so he was calling her cell. He wanted to make sure she understood that if she said anything, he would tell Maverick the truth about Candy. And for a little insurance, he thought Beth should start thinking about marriage, to him.

He made it clear he was smart enough to know

that people would question her if she suddenly changed her behaviors and they moved in together. But he was willing to let the reunion be the reason they got together, and that they didn't want to waste any more time being apart.

He announced that this coming weekend would be the perfect time for them to elope. He once again threatened her if she told anyone, and the message abruptly went dead.

Beth felt sick. She couldn't believe she was being blackmailed. And if she wanted to keep Maverick a friend, she had to do what Michael wanted.

But who knew if Maverick would even talk to her now. She hadn't heard from him since that awful argument. Even Maggie said she hadn't heard from him. Now Beth was being forced to do something against her will, again, and for the same reason: her love for Maverick and his daughter, Candy.

Finally, she said it out loud to herself, "Maverick's daughter." She'd never called her that, not to herself, and not to Maggie. Candy was the only reason she'd been able to live without him all these years. She had a part of Maverick with her. It was the best part, their love child. And Candy had his eyes, his beautiful, penetrating blue eyes.

Beth had never been overly strict on Candy, because she knew it would have done no good. She'd been like her father from the day she was born. She had been adventurous, inquisitive and curious about everything.

Alexandra had been the quiet, conservative blessing to raise. She'd inherited Robert's practical side and Beth's good looks. She and her husband had their lives all planned out. They were having their first child sometime this coming year and another one in two years. They'd traveled and bought expensive cars and boats and owned a beautiful home. Now they were ready to have children.

Candy on the other hand had traveled with the Peace Corps, had worked for UNICEF and lived in Paris, France for a couple of years studying art. She had secrets she would share with no one. Beth knew this from her childhood. She would ask odd science related questions about DNA and genes. Beth would encourage her to go ask Robert. Sometimes Candy would, and other times, she would just stare at her with her father's eyes, haunting Beth.

Maggie had once told Beth that Candy asked why her mother had named her Cadence, which meant a short military dance. Maggie had told her that her mother had been so happy to find out she was pregnant, that she'd done a little dance, but she didn't think Dance would be a nice name for a girl.

Maggie had rescued her, and Beth was grateful.

Beth had put away her freshman and sophomore yearbooks so Candy would never see that name in print. Beth had also talked Robert into attending church in another town when Candy was starting junior high so he could "network" more clients than just the ones in their small community. All of this was for

Candy's protection and Beth's own sanity.

But high school had been another thing, and Beth had taken no chances. She'd sent Candy to a private Christian School, where very few people knew Beth or her family. She'd worked hard to make sure Candy was happy and content.

She didn't invest the time, nor did she need to with Alexa. Her father gravitated to her more, becoming very involved with her, and parenting her with an intensity Candy never knew.

Beth supposed it was understandable. He'd been busy finishing school when Candy was born one month "premature." She'd always added a month to whatever due date the doctor gave her, so when she did give birth, it would appear to be a premature delivery. Since Candy was small, weighing barely five pounds, unlike Alexa who tipped the scales at seven-and-a half pounds, it had seemed reasonable. With five years difference between the girls, she and Robert had been more settled by the time Alexa had arrived. By then Robert had been making good money, and they'd been able to afford more.

Beth pulled into the drive at work and pushed her thoughts aside. She'd let her life slip by living in fear of someone finding out about her and Maverick. And now her worst fears were coming true. They'd only been together that one time, wildly and passionately, and then again the next morning right before he'd left. But that was all it took. She was living proof of that. Beth had begged God to forgive her, but she realized she'd never forgiven herself. Only by admitting part of it to Maverick had she truly felt better.

Now someone was trying to force her to live the lie to even a greater degree. She couldn't do it. Not anymore. Maverick or no Maverick, she refused to marry Michael Dunkirk or share his bed. She would call Maggie and tell her that she was right. Maybe it was time to tell the truth, the whole truth.

Better late than never, she would tell Maverick the truth.

Once in her parking spot, she dialed Maggie's number. When her friend answered, she said, "Maggie, I have some news to tell you. You'd better sit down for this."

MAGGIE HUNG UP the phone and dialed Maverick's cell. He should be coming back today, anyway, but he would flip out when he heard this.

"Cadence here."

"Maggie here."

"Hey, what's up? Anything wrong?"

"Beth asked if I would try and get hold of you." Maggie let out a long breath, and at the end, she gave a short whistle, just to pique his curiosity.

"Regarding what?"

"The truth!" Maggie couldn't hold it in. "Can you believe it? Beth said she wants to tell you the whole truth. I nearly fell out of my chair. I had to ask her to repeat it, just to make sure I wasn't hearing things."

"Well, we'll see if she does. I'm not calling or

seeing her until this weekend. This will let me know if she's really in love with me or just trying to protect Candy. I called my daughter yesterday and told her that all the plans were coming along as expected. She's so excited."

"Wonderful!" Maggie could hardly wait.

"So, you can tell Marilyn you talked to me and that I'll talk to her on Sunday. Let me know how she takes the news. I may have to change my plans. Oh, we're boarding. I'll call you when we land. Love you, Mags."

"Same here." Maggie hung up the phone, wondering what kind of game Maverick was playing.

Three hours later Maggie's phone rang. It was Maverick. "I'm back, and I've rented a car so Beth won't see mine around town. I have it parked out at the ranch. So, look for a silver BMW. That'll be me. You're going to have to trust me, Maggie, that everything will work out the way it's supposed to. I can't tell you what's going to happen, because I don't know myself. It's up to Marilyn. She's going to have to let me know how to play my hand. Just make sure that she doesn't do anything crazy between now and Saturday."

"I thought you said Sunday."

"I did. Come Sunday it will all make sense one way or another."

Maverick ended the phone conversation.

Maggie wasn't sure what to think. But she knew Beth would be upset that she couldn't talk to Maverick until Sunday. It would be difficult keeping her calmed down, especially if Michael called.

Now that Beth wanted to tell Maverick the truth, Maggie would be hard pressed to keep her away from him. The man had something more than his arm up his sleeve, and he wasn't letting anyone know what it was.

Then, of course, that was Maverick for you.

— 20 —

IT SEEMED LIKE an eternity before Saturday finally arrived. Beth had tried to contact Maverick through Maggie without success. She'd even tried to reach him once herself but wouldn't leave a message, only, "This is Marilyn."

She was growing more anxious as the weekend approached. She was determined not to let Michael or anyone else stand in the way of her living her life on her own terms.

Now that she'd decided this, a new emerging courage manifested itself in Beth, giving her hope. She wanted to be with Maverick for the rest of her life. She'd always loved him. No one else had ever claimed her heart, because he'd had it since she was thirteen.

Maverick was her soul mate. He was the man she dreamed of and yearned for in the late night and early morning hours when sleep wouldn't come. Maverick was the name she had screamed when the pangs of birth were more than she could stand.

Not once had she asked for her husband at either birth, but she had screamed and begged for Maverick when both of her daughters had come into the world.

And when things were going badly, she'd look in Candy's eyes and know that a part of Maverick was with her.

She wanted to enjoy hers and Maverick's grand-children together. She was tired of looking over her shoulder and worrying about what someone might say or do that would expose her secret.

She didn't want to live a lie anymore.

Michael had sent instructions to Beth via courier regarding the plans. Beth had directions on where to meet the scoundrel. It was a small wedding chapel about an hour away. The minister would perform the ceremony, and they would stop and get the license afterward.

The ceremony was just a formality, so questions wouldn't be raised. They'd have photographs taken, so everything would appear that this was what Beth had wanted to do. They'd then honeymoon for a week before Beth left to go to her daughter's wedding.

Michael had said she should continue with the plans she had made so as not to arouse suspicion. But he made it very clear that he would destroy her, Maverick, and her daughter if he was in any way endangered or exposed.

For insurance, he sent a picture of her daughter with her fiancé smiling from her post in Greenland.

Beth knew Michael had to have connections to be able to obtain a photograph she didn't have, and she was confident he wasn't making an idle or hollow promise.

So it was with extreme caution that she drove toward her destination. Her heart pounded almost out of her chest. Her mouth was dry. She tried her best to think of exactly how she was going to tell him: No matter what, she would never marry Michael Dunkirk. Whatever the outcome between her and Maverick, she wouldn't be bullied and blackmailed. She'd told Maggie to wait for her call, and if she didn't receive it, for Maggie to contact the police.

When Beth arrived, she was surprised at how cute the wedding chapel looked. It was like a page from a fairy tale. It was a church with old-fashioned shutters and stained-glass windows, with a small bridge in the front over a narrow creek. The outside of the building was lined with beautiful pink roses and white lilies set in pots at the front door.

A lattice archway covered with greenery and roses stood near the entrance.

Beth's nervousness didn't let her enjoy any of the charm. She had to be strong enough to get this over with. After stopping the car, she got out, locked the door, and straightened her clothing. With newfound inner resolve, she walked with a straight back over the bridge and onto the porch. She put her hand on the antique doorknob and prayed she would be brave enough to follow through with her plans.

Once inside, the chapel was filled with fresh flowers, twinkling lights, and iridescent gossamer covering everything. It was breathtaking. She couldn't believe Michael would have taken so much care in planning this farce of a wedding.

A gentleman approached who identified himself as the minister. Then she heard a cough, and coming out of a side room was Michael. He was dressed wearing a white suit. He walked toward Beth, and her knees began to shake. Michael reached out and took her hand.

"Beth, honey, why didn't you wear a wedding dress?" he asked sweetly.

Beth glanced at her simple summer dress and sandals and into his face. "Because I don't plan on getting married," she said in an unsteady voice.

"What? I don't believe I heard you correctly." He sounded angry.

"You heard me." Beth spoke in a flat, defeated tone. She took a deep breath and continued. "I made a mistake when I was young. I was pregnant with Maverick's baby, the only man I've ever loved. I should have waited for him. But I was afraid of my father. He'd already threatened me about Maverick when I was younger, saying he would send me away to a boarding school. If he knew I was pregnant by Maverick, he'd have made me give up the baby for adoption. I could've never given up our child. Maverick's baby was all I had to live for.

"So I did the best I could and slept with Robert one time so I could tell him I was pregnant. That was my crime, loving my baby and her father. But I won't be threatened by you. My father almost ruined my life; I won't let you, Michael Dunkirk, ruin the rest of it. So, if you think telling Maverick will bring you some sadistic satisfaction, then go ahead. He doesn't love me, anyway. But you won't hurt his daughter or destroy her happiness. I'll kill you myself before she has to live what I've been through. I won't marry you. That's final!"

Beth let out a sigh and dropped, exhausted, on the pew next to where they'd been standing at the back of the chapel. *God,* she sent up in a desperate cry, *why have you let me come to this?* She was shaking, but she refused to cry.

"Was that what you wanted?" Michael asked, looking behind Beth. Beth turned, and there stood Maverick, her Maverick. All the breath went out of her body, and a chill ran over her.

"Yes, that's exactly what I wanted to hear," Maverick said hoarsely, with tears coming to his eyes. "That's all I've ever wanted to hear." He stood staring at Beth, who was still in a state of shock at knowing what Maverick had just overheard. No one spoke for several minutes. Maverick continued to stare at Beth, with a smile on his face and happiness in his eyes.

Finally, Michael spoke up. "We had a deal, remember?"

"Yes, I remember. You get to live another day. But if you ever come near her or make her feel uncomfortable in any way, you'll wish you'd gone to prison instead, got it? God has tied my hands, telling me I can't punch you in the face, but if you come around again, I'll see if God will give me permission to do more. Do I make myself clear?"

"Crystal," Michael's replied.

It was then Beth noticed the make-up Michael was wearing to cover the shiner he had under his left eye. She'd been so nervous she hadn't noticed anything but his white suit. Maverick nodded affirmatively in Michael's direction and waited as he headed toward the exit. He muttered as he left that he was leaving the state and would never return.

Beth wiped her frustration from her eyes and turned to Maverick. "You knew about this and didn't try to help me? You were going to let me go through with this?"

Maverick carefully pulled Beth up and stood facing her with his hand under her chin. He lifted her face gently so she could see only him. He spoke in a soft, low tone so only she heard him.

"Why do you think I'm here, Marilyn? I trusted God to work out the problems between us, and this is the way he showed me. I had to know the truth once and for all. I had to know that you loved me back then as much as I love you right now. I had to know there was hope for a future with you. As soon as I figured out who it was that had hurt you, I went after him. Michael was more than happy to cooperate rather than spend time in prison. He told me everything he knew. But I'm the one who sent you the courier package." He paused, and then said, "And yes, I'm the one who sent you the picture of our daughter."

"I've prayed for the same thing. I've so wanted to be with you again." Beth felt lightheaded, and that was all she remembered until she heard Maverick questioning her.

"Marilyn, honey, are you okay? Maggie, give her some more water to drink."

Beth slowly opened her eyes. She was still in the wedding chapel, and only Maggie was with them. She didn't remember fainting.

"What's Maggie doing here?" she asked, puzzled, unaware she was lying in Maverick's arms on the floor.

"I've come to be the witness." Maggie giggled softly. "I'm thankful you're coming around from your fainting spell."

"Witness to what?" Beth became aware of Maverick's arms around her.

"Marilyn, you fainted when I told you about the photograph I had of Candy and Drew. I caught you in my arms as you went down. Maggie was just coming in the chapel when it happened. She brought you a cup of water from the fountain. And here you are," Maverick whispered tenderly, as he looked into the emerald eyes of the woman he had waited a lifetime for.

Beth was still alarmed by the events that had just occurred. How did Maverick know about Candy, and how long had he known? Beth started to speak, but Maverick interrupted her.

"Did you mean what you said about loving me? Do you want to spend the rest of your life with your Maverick, Mary Elizabeth Monroe Taylor?"

It was the first time he'd ever called her by her true name. She smiled just thinking about it. She'd fantasized about how wonderful it would be to be with Maverick forever, without any secrets. She felt calm and serene, more at peace than she could ever remember.

"Well, baby girl." Maverick sounded slightly anxious. "Do you?"

Beth felt her face warm that she hadn't answered him. "Yes, I want to marry you, Maverick Dillinger Cadence. I want to be with you every minute of every day for the rest of my life."

"Well then, Maggie, help her get dressed. We've got a wedding to attend to," Maverick said excitedly.

Again, Beth was confused by everything. "Whose wedding and what dress?" Beth looked to Maverick for answers.

"Our wedding!" Maverick grinned from ear to ear. "In case you didn't notice, the entire wedding chapel was done to your taste and with you in mind. All the flowers, decorations, everything was chosen by Maggie for our wedding. She just didn't know when it would be. I hinted it might be when we went on the Alaskan cruise next week. So, she innocently helped me out. But the wedding dress was all me. All I needed was your size and a few alterations from a borrowed dress I took from your closet the first night you fell asleep." Maverick grinned, seeing Beth's eyes widen at his disclosure.

"You mean you planned to marry me all along?" Beth wasn't sure she understood him correctly.

"Yes, Marilyn. I was hoping we could start our lives where we left off, still crazy for each other, but this time with God in control. I know my heart hasn't changed. I just wanted to know that you in some small way felt the same, too. After talking with Maggie and Candy, I dared to hope that we could have a chance. I hoped I had the possibility of being one of the luckiest guys on the face of the earth."

She nearly cried when she saw Maggie approaching with the most beautiful mermaid-style sequined wedding dress she'd ever seen. "You mean right now? I don't have my makeup, or shoes, or my hair done." Beth felt panicked as Maverick helped her to her feet.

Maggie piped in, "I brought everything you need, and it's in the bridal chamber."

Maverick said reverently, "I don't plan to ever lose you again, baby girl." He pulled her to him and gave her a long, passionate kiss, taking her breath away, as she melted right into his arms. "And I can't wait another week to make you mine," Maverick almost growled. "Hurry!" he yelled out as Maggie led her away.

When Beth opened the bridal chamber door, Lily, Maverick's mother, was sitting there.

"I wondered how long you would make him wait this time. I knew you loved him when I heard how you wanted to keep his baby. But I already had my suspicions years ago when you married so quickly after he shipped out.

"Then, I saw your little girl when she was about three or so, and I knew she was Maverick's. She looked just like him. I saw her again when she was about ten. I had tears in my eyes when I wrote him about her. And when they put her picture in the paper as the valedictorian of her private school, I mailed the paper to Maverick. He's known for years. But when his little Cathy died, he finally had the gumption to do something about it. He finally contacted her." Lily paused for a moment, watching Beth's startled expression about the revelation of the news.

It was Maggie's turn to come clean with Beth, once Lily started it. "Candy told me she was relieved to find out Robert wasn't her father. She told me she'd always known something wasn't quite right. Since she was a little girl, she'd been allergic to milk products, and no one else in her family was. Also, Robert's eyes were brown, and yours were green. Candy knew there was no way she could have blue eyes. She never questioned you, but along with her biology professors, she sure did ask me a lot of questions. When she finally met Maverick, it answered a lot of inquiries she had about herself."

Then Lily continued, "When she and Colt met, they immediately knew they were brother and sister. We all had a wonderful time in Hawaii getting better acquainted. The only one missing was you. You've been a stubborn one. But now that you're getting married, we can finally be one big happy family on our Alaskan cruise."

Beth froze. "You mean everyone's going?" She thought she'd heard Maverick mention it earlier to Maggie.

Lily replied, smiling slyly, "Yes, Candy and her daddy planned this six months ago. They had to so Colt could put in for his time off. Candy said she especially wanted her brother to meet her mom. He doesn't know everything yet, because we weren't sure about you. But you know what they say, all's well that ends well."

Beth was totally astonished by this new information coming from the oldest member of the of the Cadence family. Everyone had known about her well-guarded secret, but no one had said anything to upset her. No wonder her daughter had wanted her to loosen up. She'd known Maverick for the past ten years, and they'd schemed together the past few months to get Maverick back into Beth's life without too much stress on her. They did all this out of love for her.

It brought tears to Beth's eyes. She would be

thankful to marry a man who loved her that much and to be a complete family with a daughter and a son.

Maggie helped Beth put on the lace-and-sequin-covered form-fitting dress. Maverick whistled, describing her as a vision of loveliness as she walked down the aisle and repeated her vows, holding a beautiful bouquet of soft pink roses and white lilies with Lily softly crying to see her son finally happy. And when the rings were exchanged, a five-carat diamond was placed on Beth's slender finger, while a plain gold band was given to Maverick. The minister ended the ceremony with a prayer for guidance that God would keep his hand on every aspect of the couple's new life together. Maggie smiled with tears in her eyes to finally see what should have happened forty years ago.

After the pictures were taken, the marriage license was obtained, and it was officially signed, Maverick said, "I have a confession to make."

"What?" Beth wondered what secrets he could possibly have.

"Let's wait until we get to the hotel. I want to make up for some lost time." He winked, and this time Beth didn't blush. Instead, she nodded yes and snuggled close to him, giving Maverick even more reason to get to the hotel immediately.

— Epilogue —

SEVERAL HOURS LATER, Beth and Maverick lay together on the first night of their honeymoon, totally relaxed and complete in one another's arms.

Beth shyly said, "It was worth the wait. After almost forty years, it was better than I remembered."

Maverick totally agreed, as he kissed her hair and held her close.

Beth whispered, "I haven't forgotten you had something to confess." She rested her hand on his chest, as she nestled against him. "What's the confession you have to make?"

Maverick looked a little sheepish, with his boyish appearance piquing Beth's curiosity.

"Candy had wanted us to get married aboard the ship along with her and Drew. But I knew I couldn't wait another day, much less a week to make you mine. Marilyn, do you think a week would be too soon to renew our vows?" Maverick grinned.

"Not if we can have a second honeymoon." Beth smiled seductively.

"The first one's not over yet," Maverick said, as he pulled Beth to him again.

Did you like this book?

There's more!

Read all three books in **The Reunion Series** by
DeLora Conley-Walls.

Trusting Heart Reunion

(Out Now!)

Timeless Heart Reunion

(Out Now!)

True Heart Reunion

(Coming Summer 2018!)

Find these and more at:

THREE SKILLET
www.ThreeSkilletPublishing.com

and

Amazon